SKATEBOARD SONAR

WITHDRAWN
WATERFORD CITY AND COUNTY

SPORTS ZONE
SPECIAL REPORT

SKT
SKATEBOARDING

PNT
PAINTBALL

FBL
FOOTBALL

BSL
BASEBALL

BBL
BASKETBALL

HKY
HOCKEY

BLIND SKATER COMPETES FOR STREET COURSE TITLE!

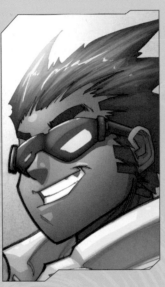

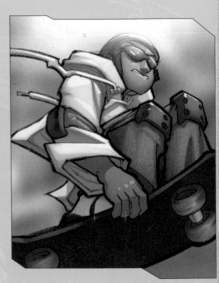

MATTHEW LYONS

STATS:
NICKNAME: MATTY
AGE: 13
EVENT: STREET

BIO: Matty is blind, but you wouldn't know it from watching him skate – he has become a top-notch street course skater despite his disability. Matty has also developed a reputation as a local hero for his difficult grabs, stellar tricks and positive attitude. Matty is usually seen with his skateboard and his best buddy, Ty, nearby.

Sports Illustrated KIDS

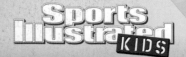

UP NEXT: SKATEBOARD SONAR

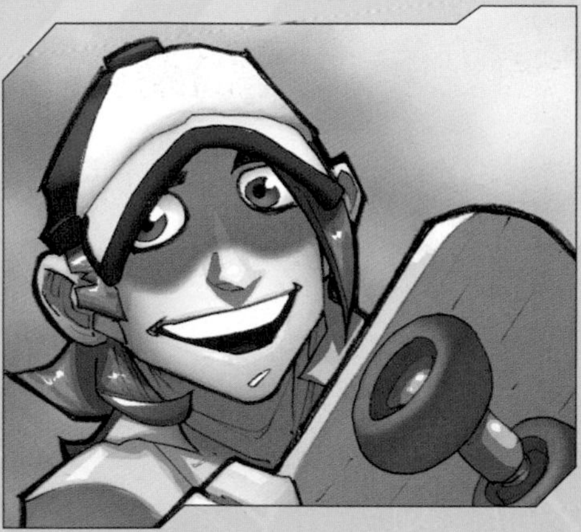

TYSON TAGGART

NICKNAME: TY

AGE: 13 EVENT: HALFPIPE

BIO: Ty is a hot-head who reigns supreme on the halfpipe. He skates hard and loves to put on a good show. Ty has been best friends with Matty Lyons since kindergarten.

BLZ vs BKS 3-1
TGR vs RDR 33-32
EAG vs BAN 14-7
SPA vs WLD 4-3
BAN vs RDR 21-15
RZR vs LIG 4-3
BLZ vs BKS 3-1

CLINTON WASHBURN

NICKNAME: CLINT AGE: 13 EVENT: HALFPIPE

BIO: Clint's a talented boarder who's trouble on – and off – the halfpipe. His best buddy is the big bully, Bing Hawtin.

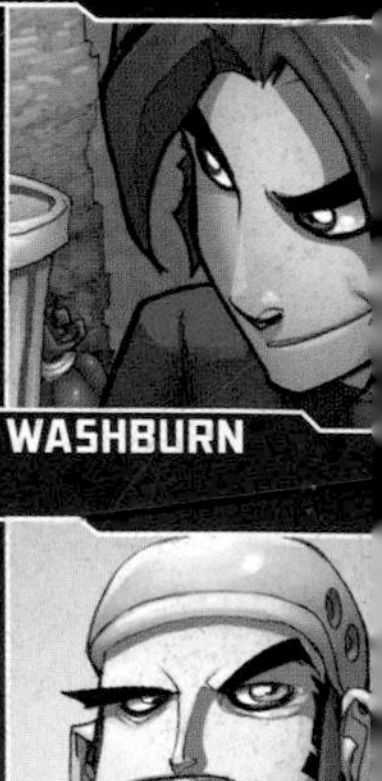

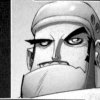

WASHBURN

BINGLEY HAWTIN

NICKNAME: BING AGE: 14 EVENT: STREET

BIO: The only thing Bing likes to do more than pick on puny skaters is beat them senseless on the street course.

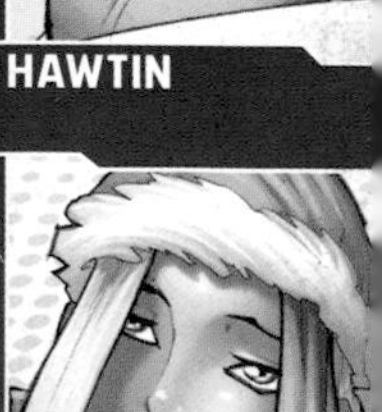

HAWTIN

JILLIAN SPEARS

NICKNAME: JILLY AGE: 17 JOB: PARK OWNER

BIO: Jilly's a true patron of the skating art. A talented skater herself, Jilly's park will host the All-City Skating Competition.

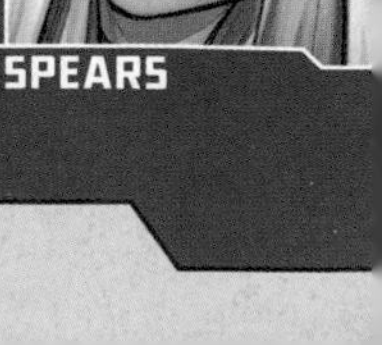

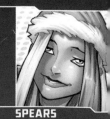

SPEARS

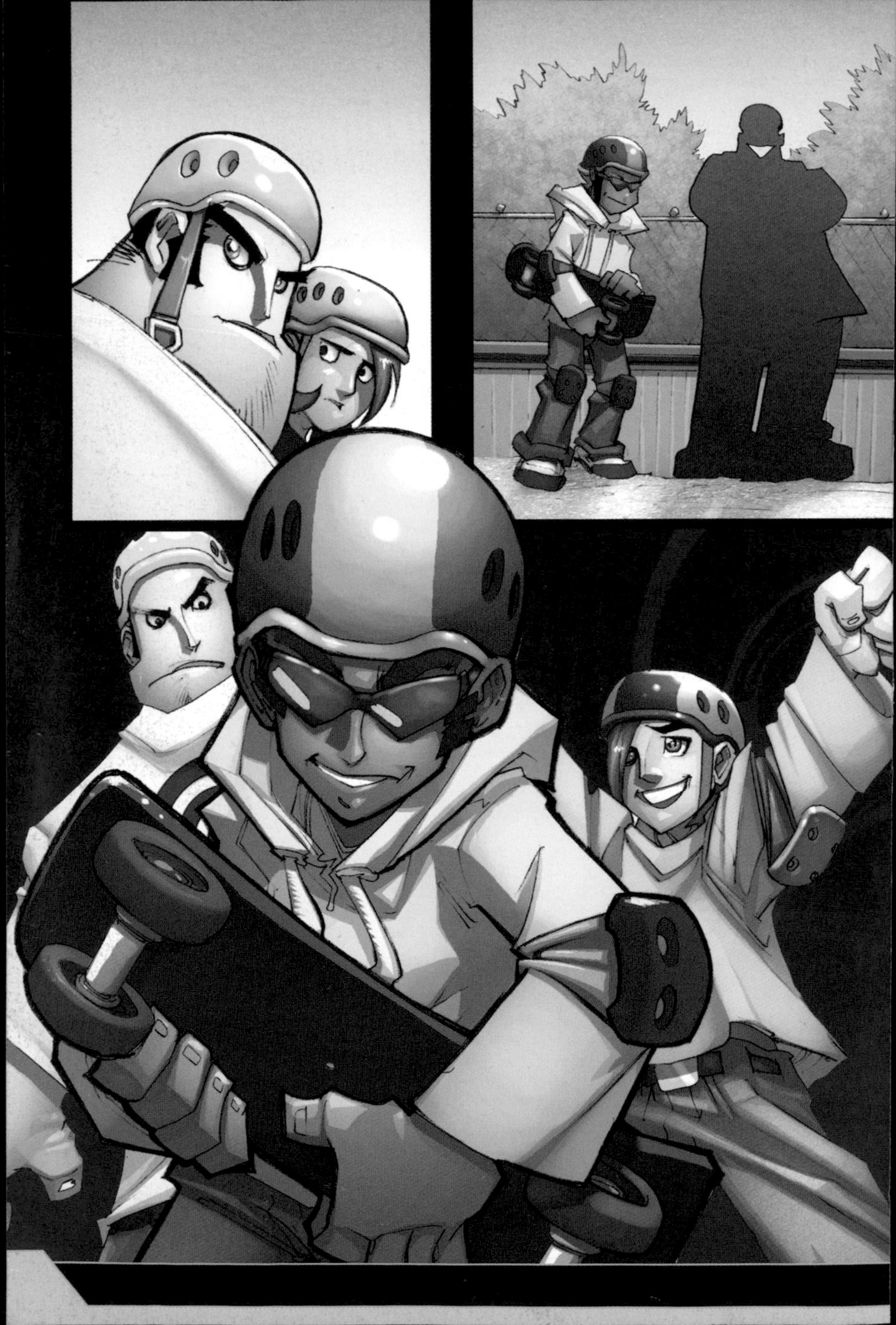

Sports Illustrated KIDS

PRESENTS

SKATEBOARD SONAR

A PRODUCTION OF

raintree

a Capstone company — publishers for children

written by *Eric Stevens*
illustrated by *Gerardo Sandoval*
coloured by *Benny Fuentes*

designed and directed by *Bob Lentz*
edited by *Sean Tulien*
creative direction by *Heather Kindseth*
editorial direction by *Michael Dahl*

Raintree is an imprint of Capstone Global Library, a company incorporated in England and Wales having its registered office at 264 Banbury Road, Oxford, OX2 7DY – Registered company number: 6695582

www.raintree.co.uk
myorders@raintree.co.uk

Text © Capstone Global Library Limited 2019
The moral rights of the proprietor have been asserted.

ISBN: 978 1 4747 7157 3
22 21 20 19 18
10 9 8 7 6 5 4 3 2

British Library Cataloguing in Publication Data
A full catalogue record for this book is available from the British Library.

Originated by Capstone Global Library Ltd
Printed and bound in India

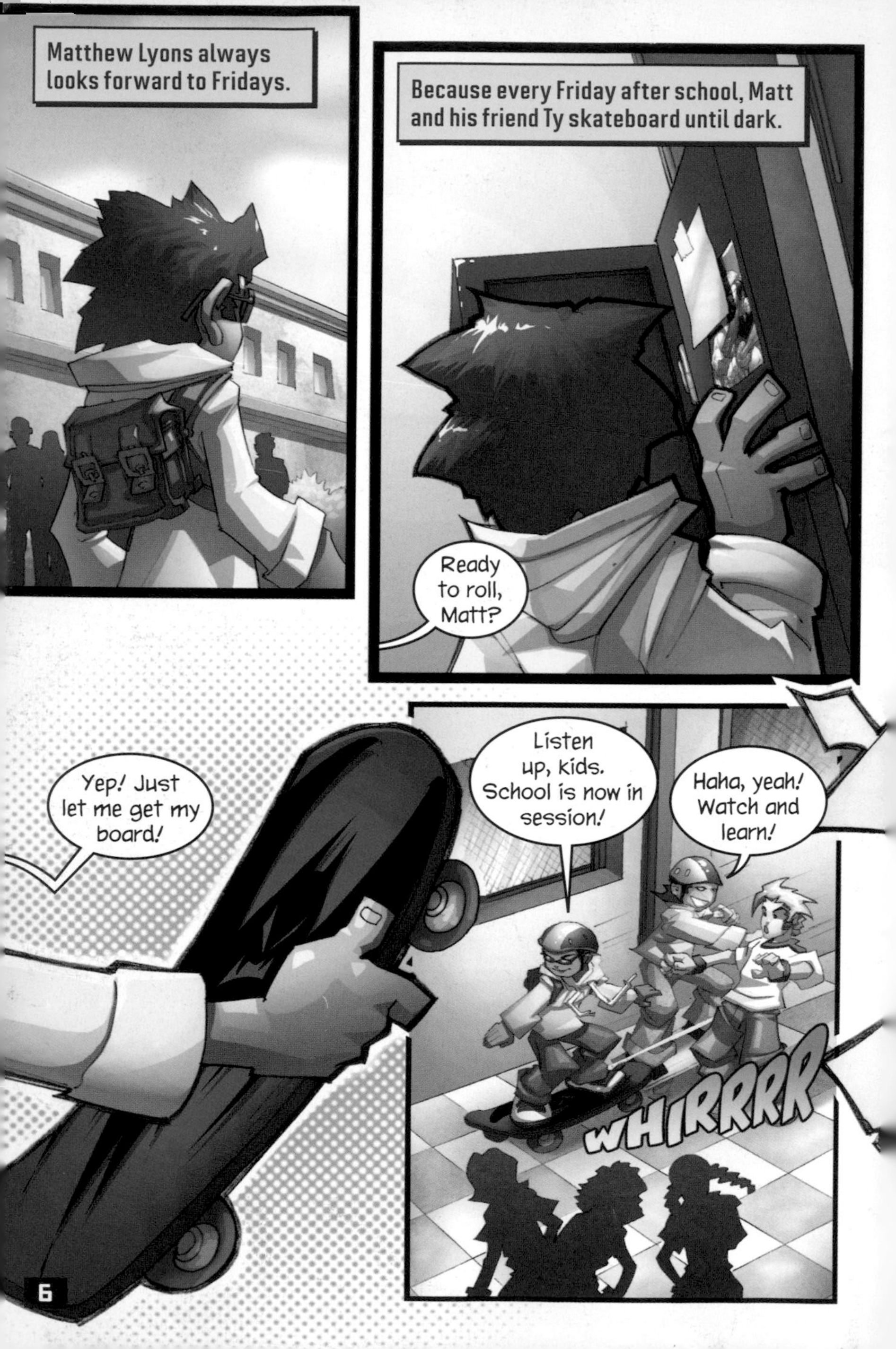

Matthew Lyons always looks forward to Fridays.
Because every Friday after school, Matt and his friend Ty skateboard until dark.
Ready to roll, Matt?
Yep! Just let me get my board!
Listen up, kids. School is now in session!
Haha, yeah! Watch and learn!
WHIRRRR

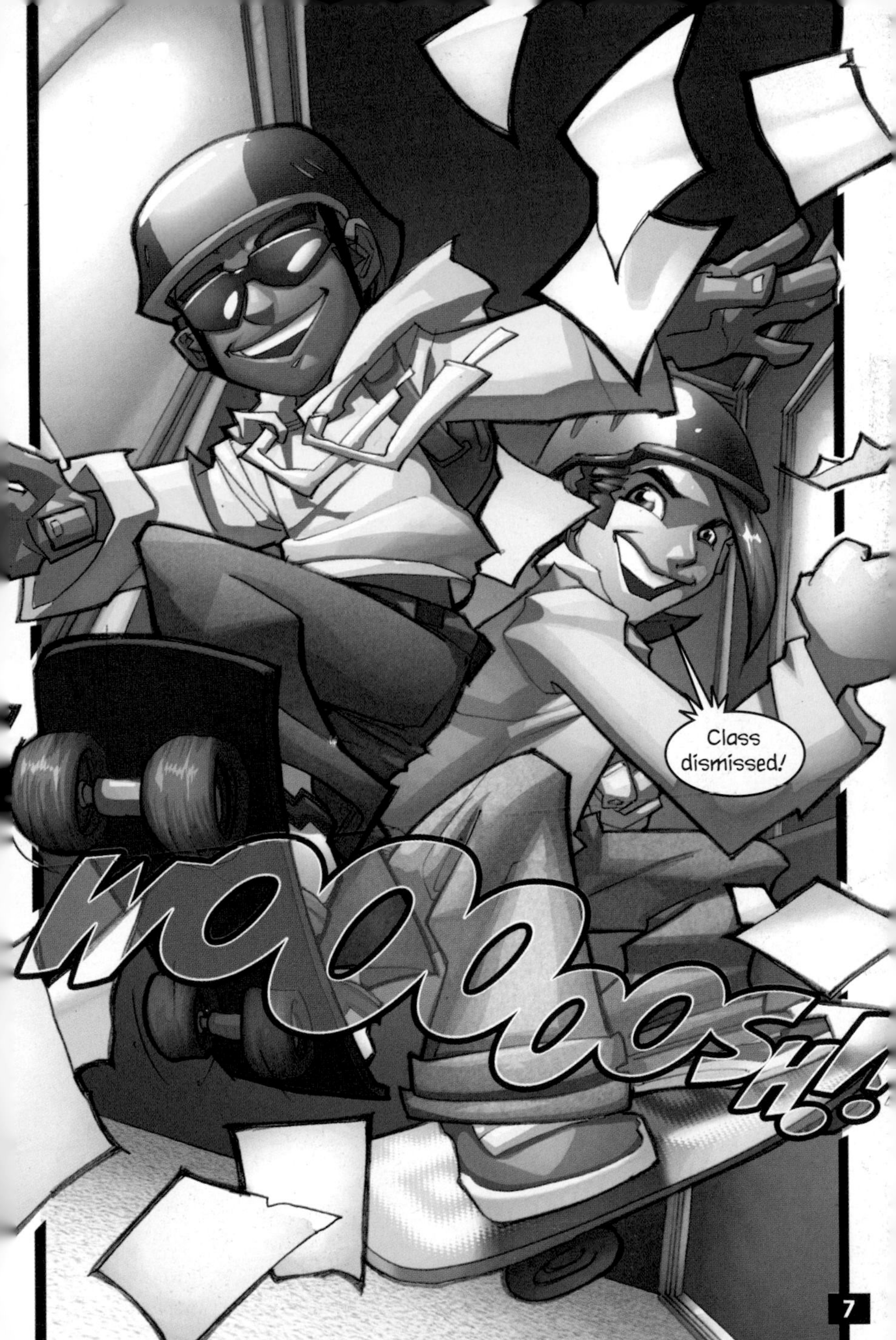
Class dismissed!
WHOOOOSH!!

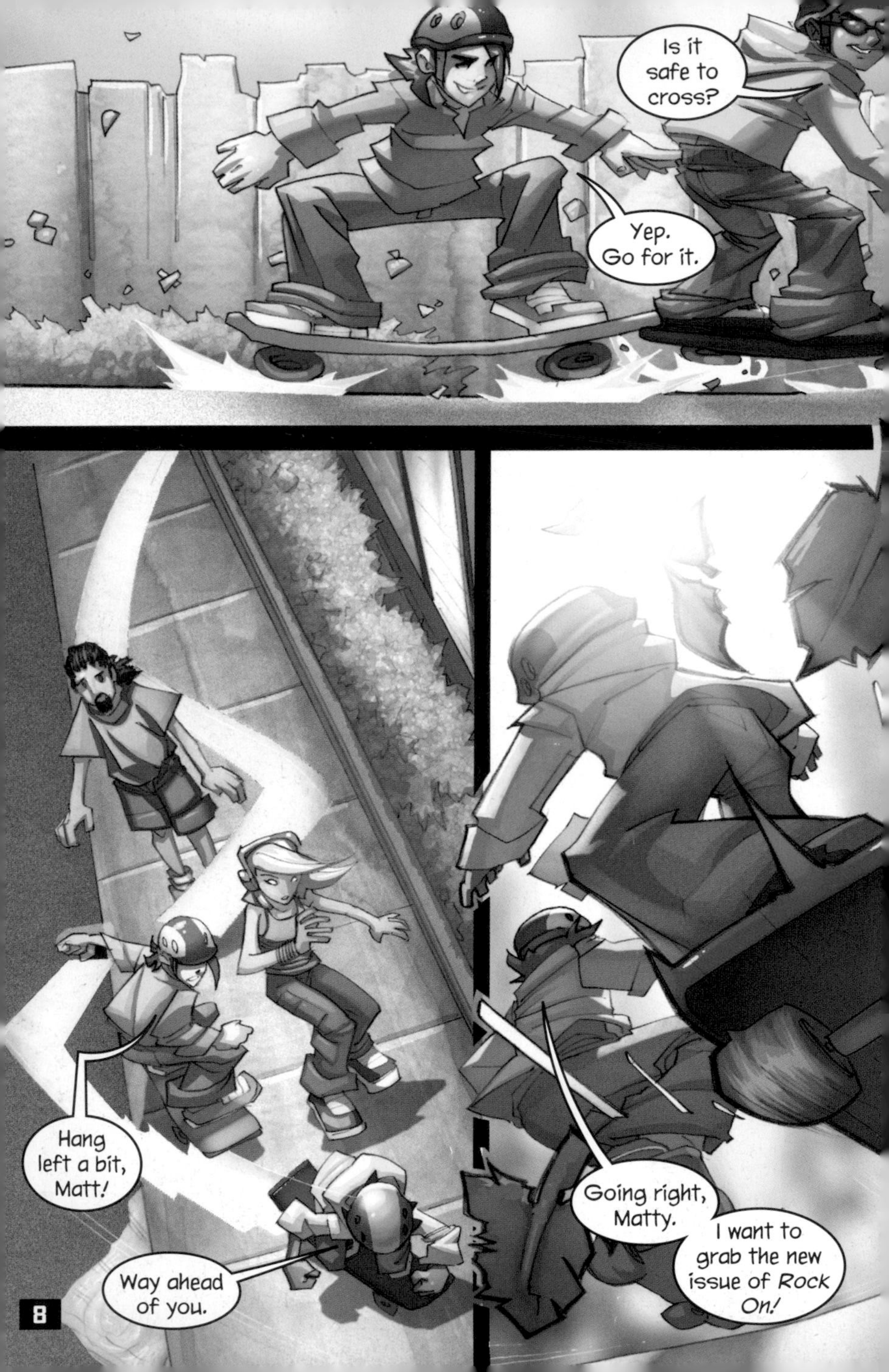
Is it safe to cross?
Yep. Go for it.
Hang left a bit, Matt!
Way ahead of you.
Going right, Matty.
I want to grab the new issue of *Rock On!*

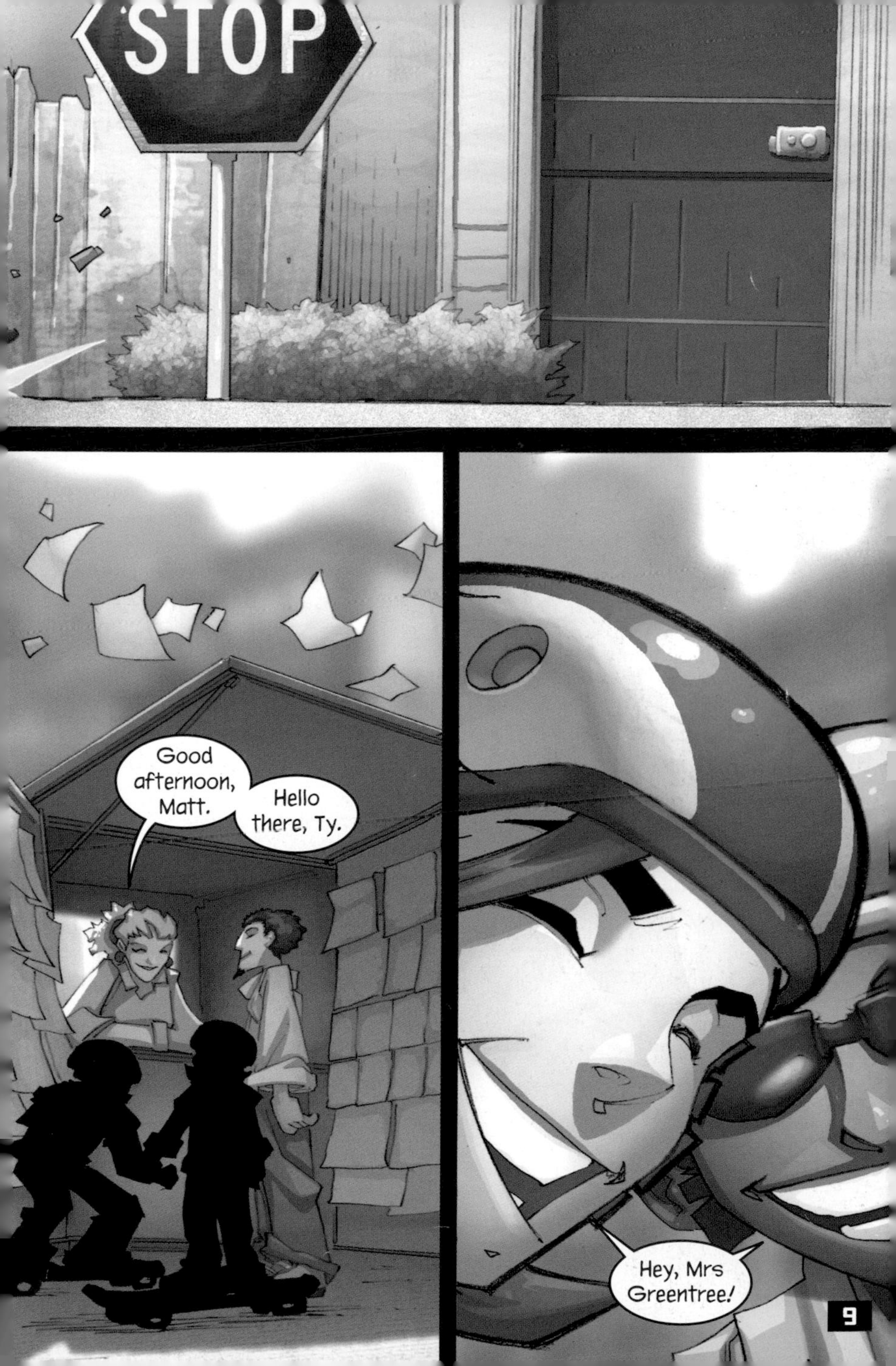
STOP
Good afternoon, Matt.
Hello there, Ty.
Hey, Mrs Greentree!

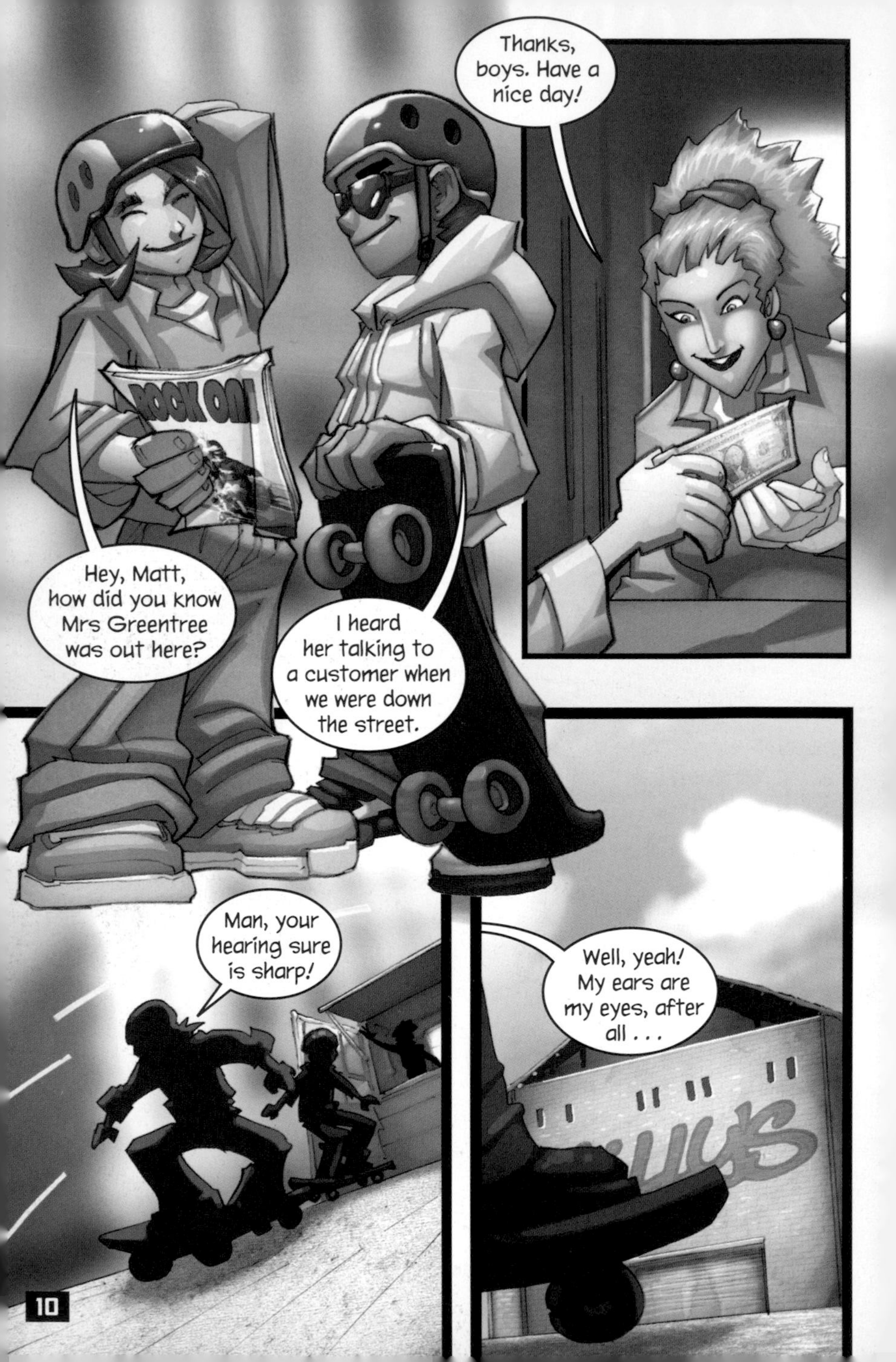
ROCK ON!
Thanks, boys. Have a nice day!
Hey, Matt, how did you know Mrs Greentree was out here?
I heard her talking to a customer when we were down the street.
Man, your hearing sure is sharp!
Well, yeah! My ears are my eyes, after all . . .

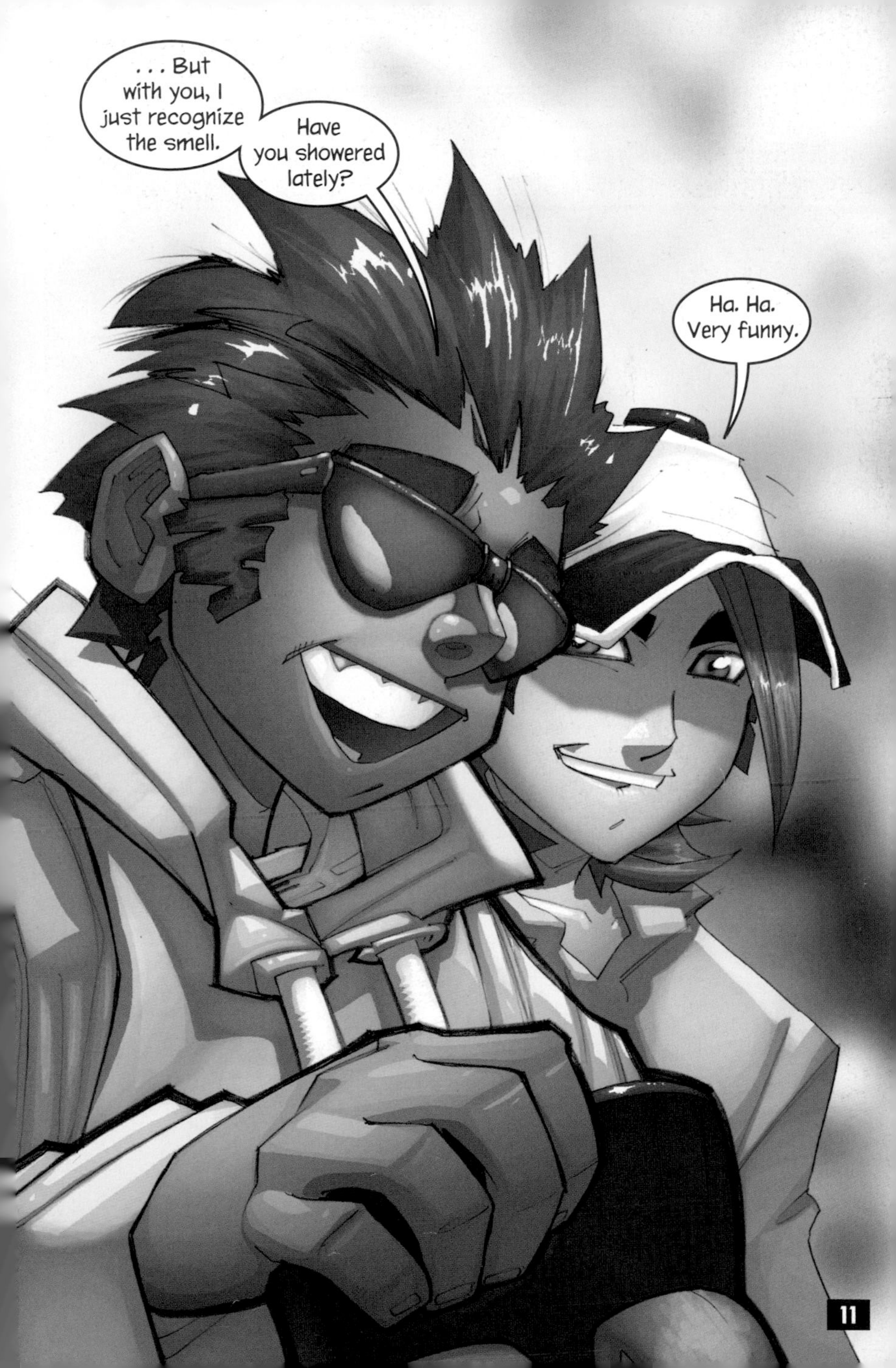
. . . But with you, I just recognize the smell.
Have you showered lately?
Ha. Ha. Very funny.

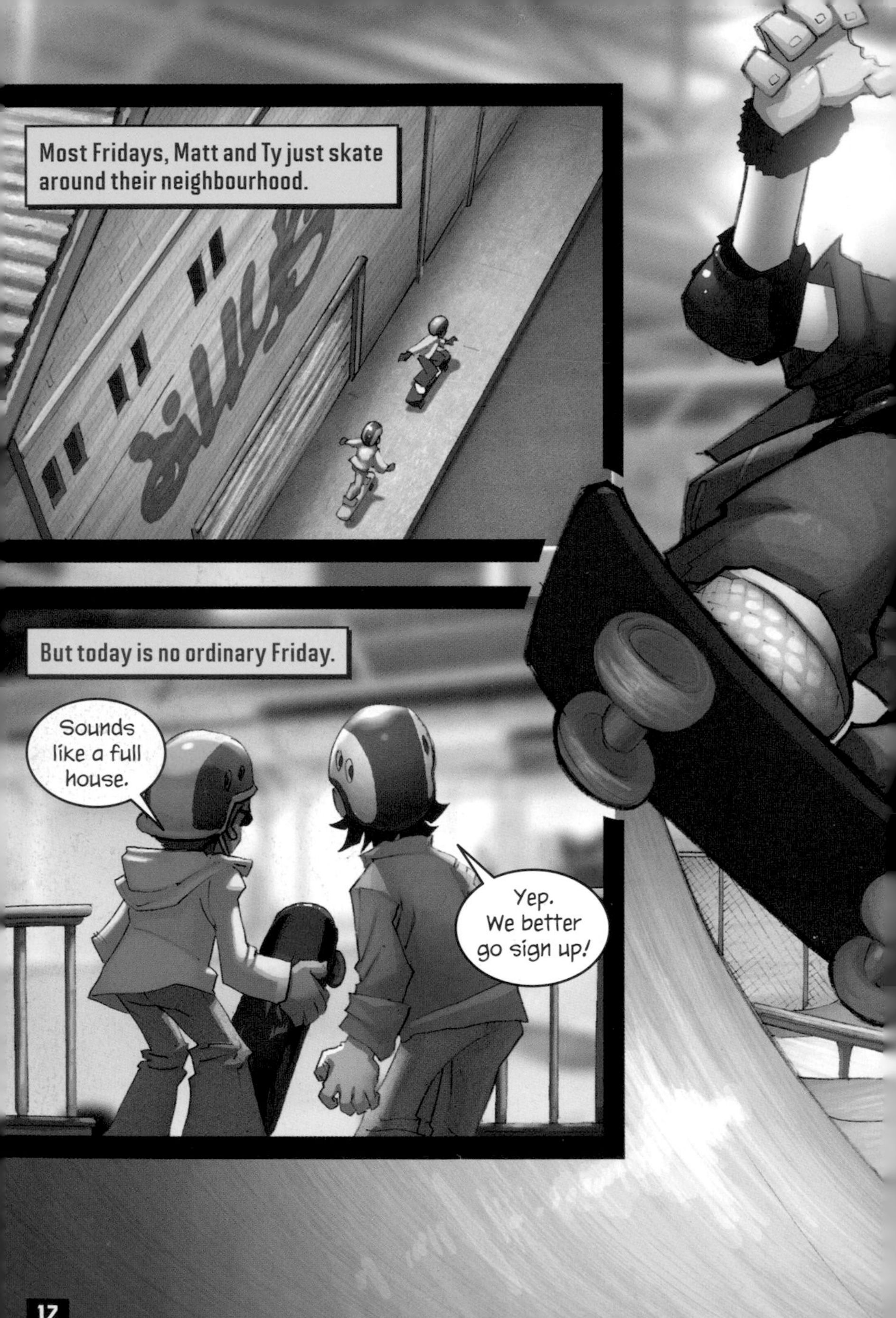
Most Fridays, Matt and Ty just skate around their neighbourhood.
But today is no ordinary Friday.
Sounds like a full house.
Yep. We better go sign up!

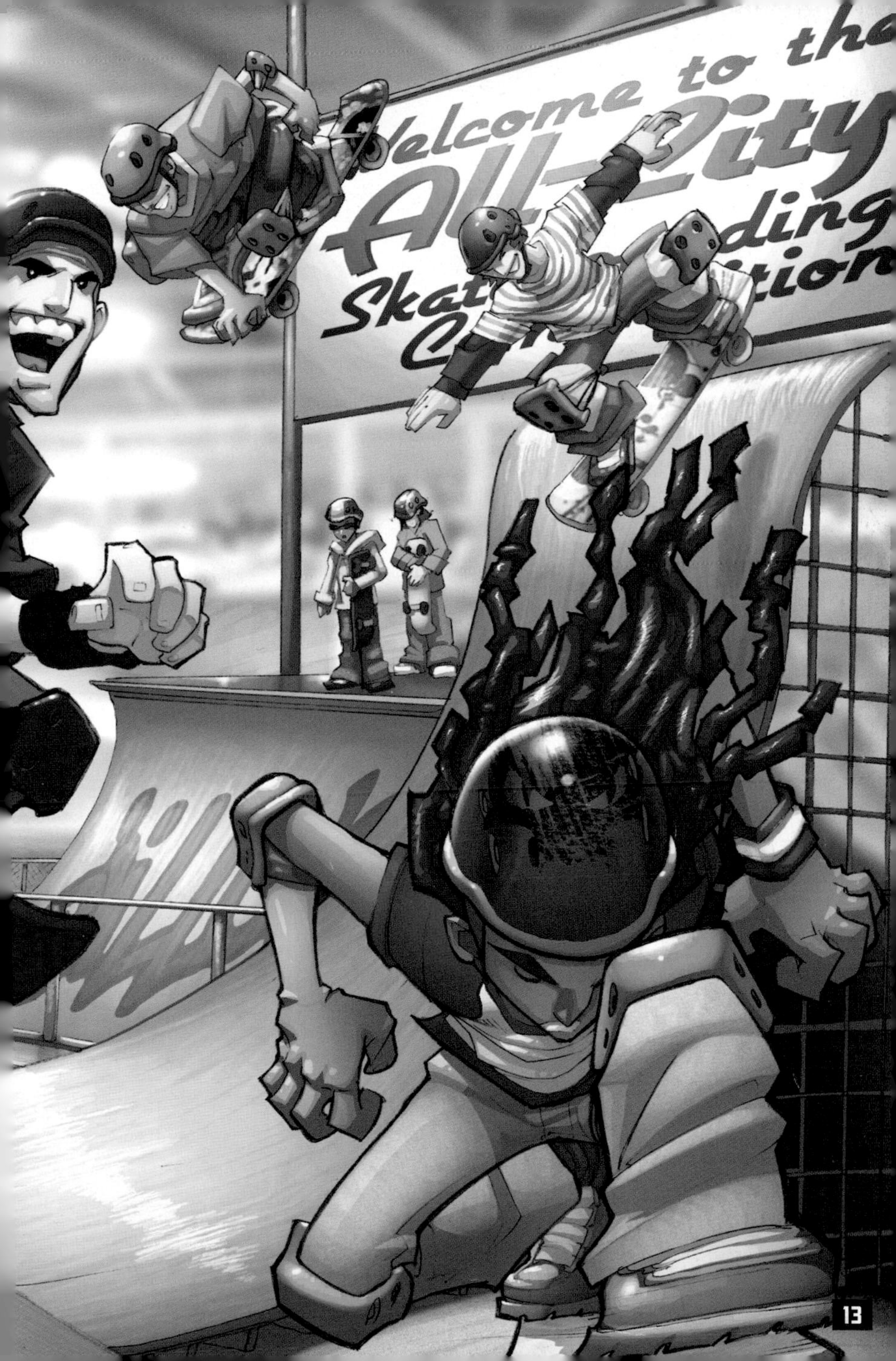
Welcome to the

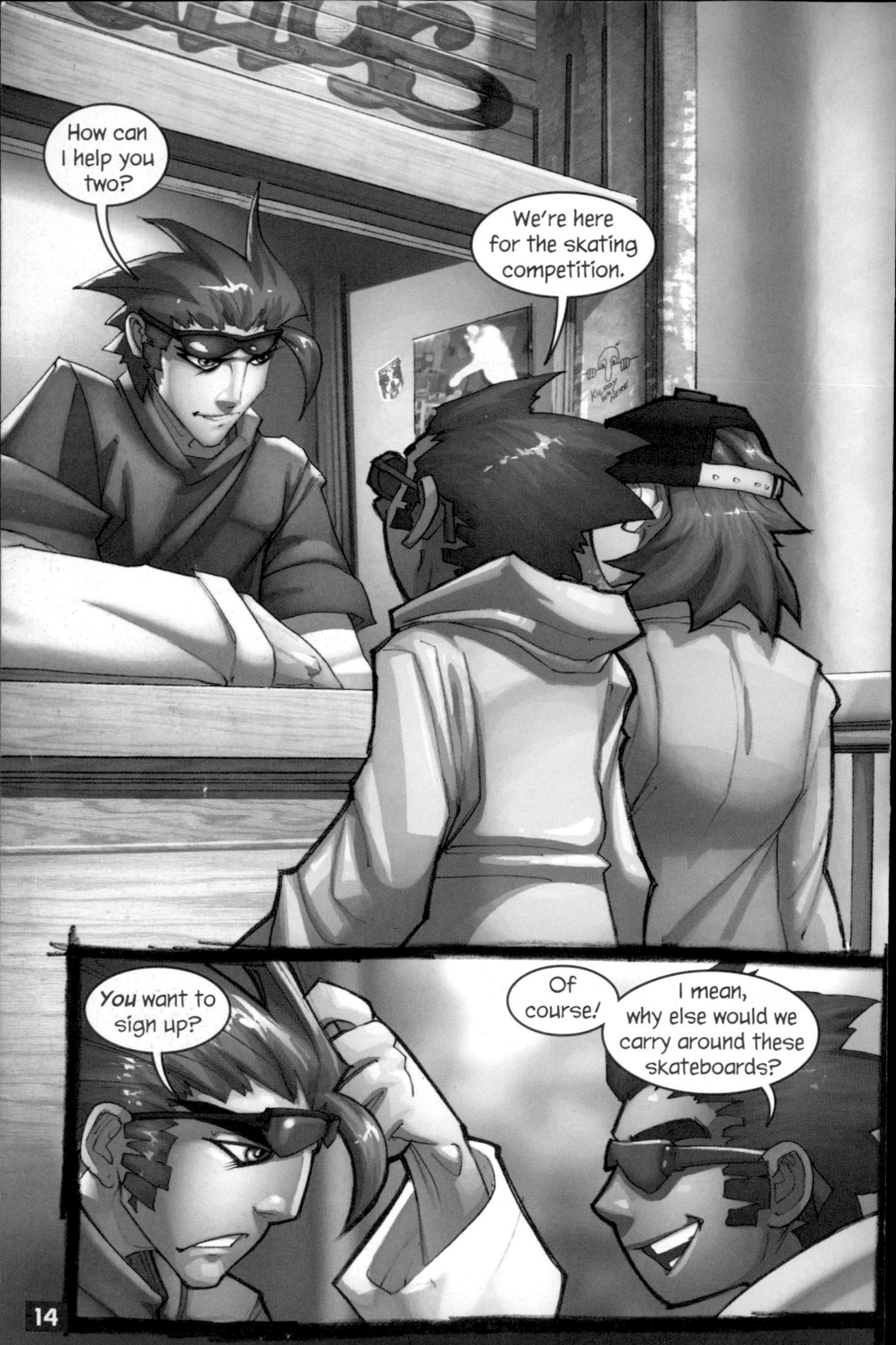
How can I help you two?
We're here for the skating competition.
KILROY WAS HERE
You want to sign up?
Of course!
I mean, why else would we carry around these skateboards?

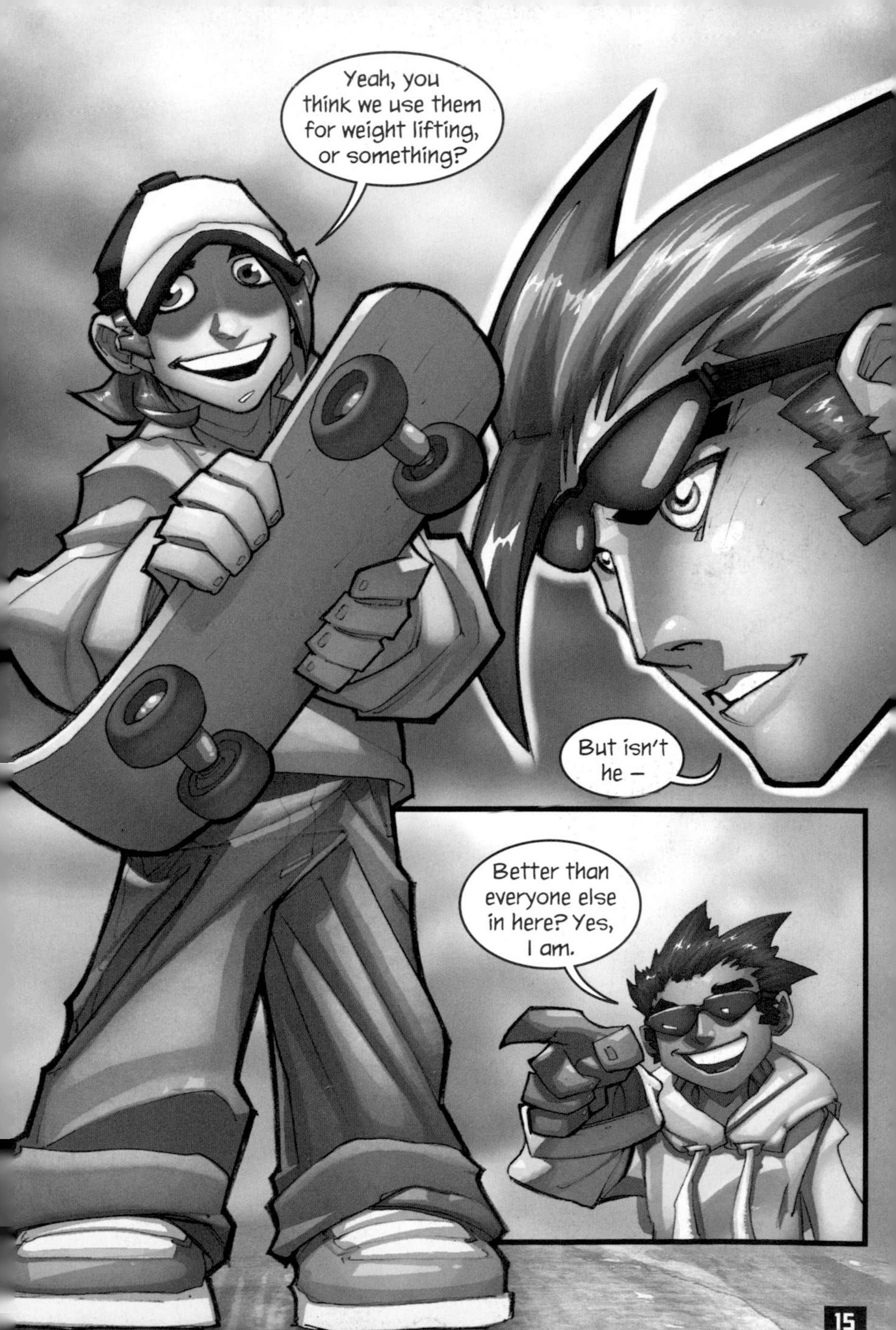
Yeah, you think we use them for weight lifting, or something?
But isn't he –
Better than everyone else in here? Yes, I am.

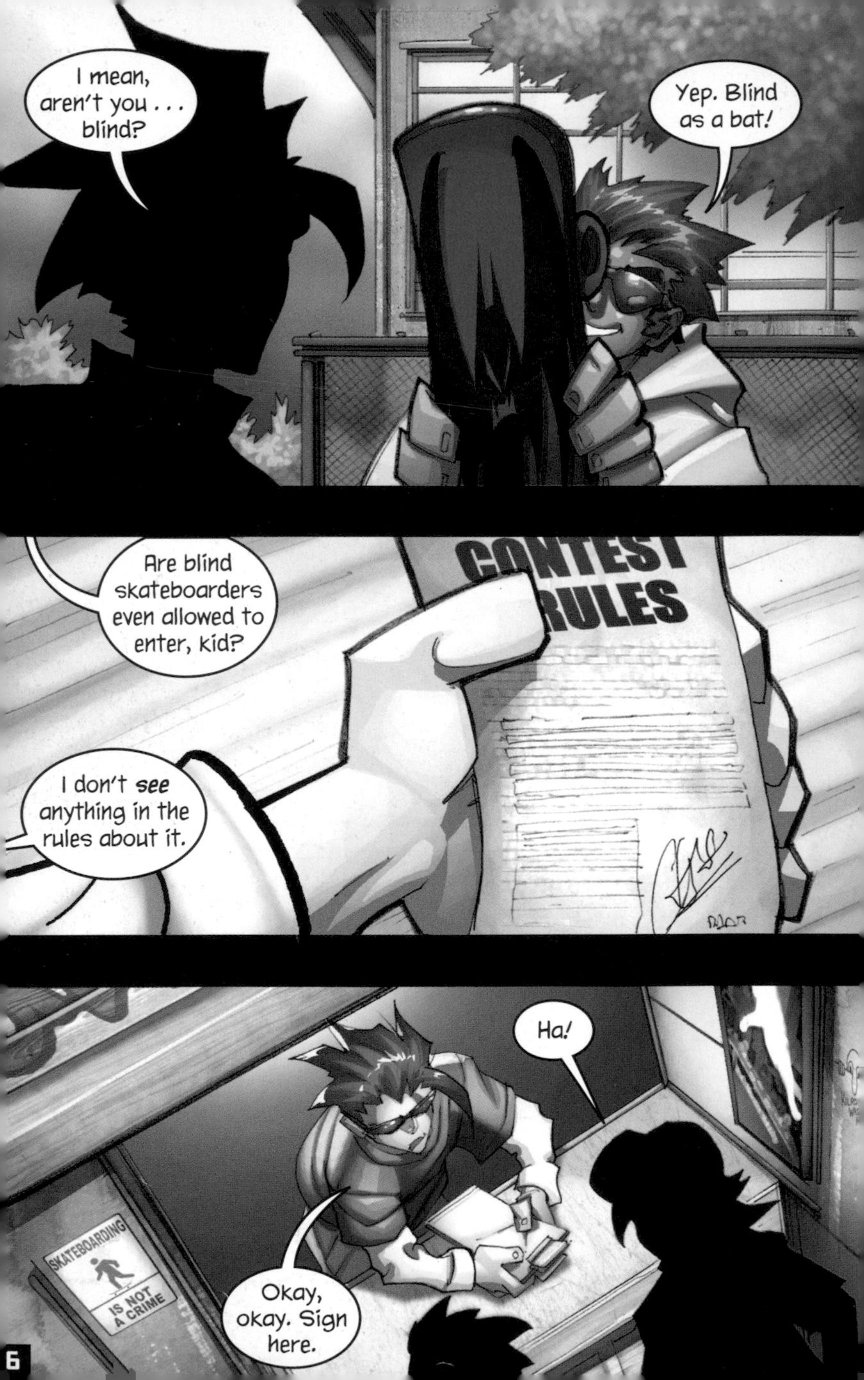
I mean, aren't you . . . blind?
Yep. Blind as a bat!
CONTEST RULES
Are blind skateboarders even allowed to enter, kid?
I don't *see* anything in the rules about it.
Ha!
SKATEBOARDING IS NOT A CRIME
Okay, okay. Sign here.

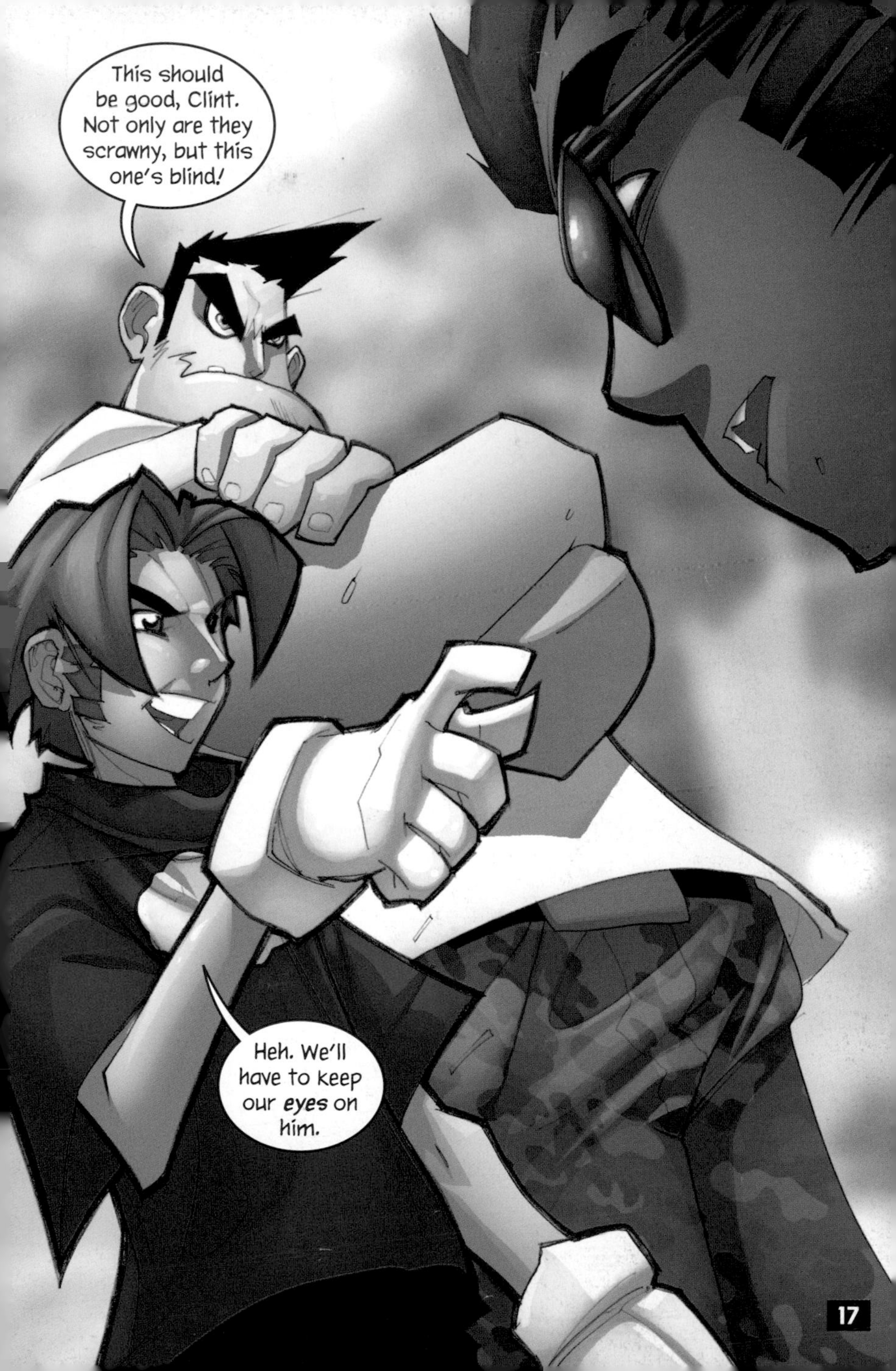
This should be good, Clint. Not only are they scrawny, but this one's blind!
Heh. We'll have to keep our *eyes* on him.

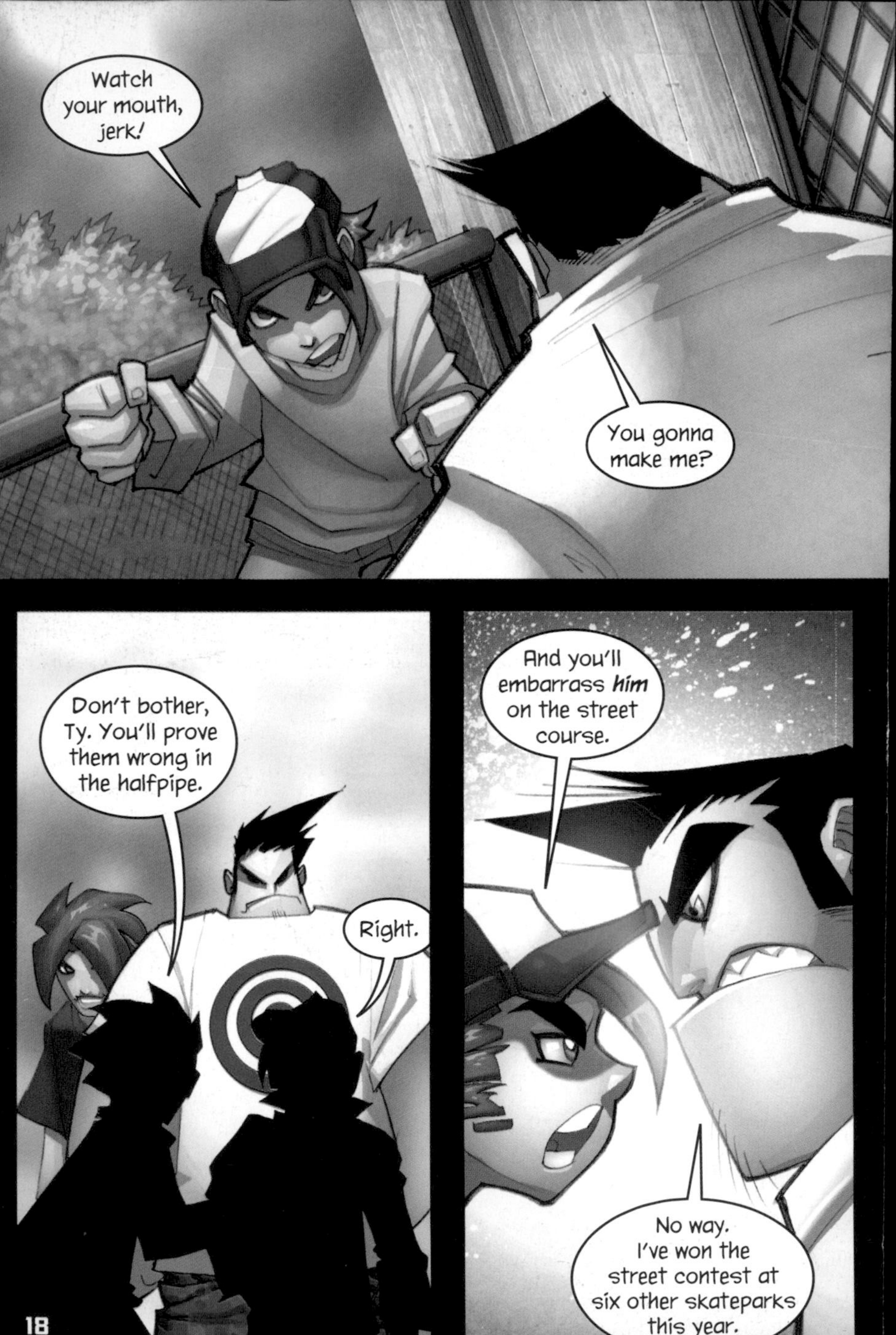

Watch your mouth, jerk!
You gonna make me?
Don't bother, Ty. You'll prove them wrong in the halfpipe.
Right.
And you'll embarrass *him* on the street course.
No way. I've won the street contest at six other skateparks this year.

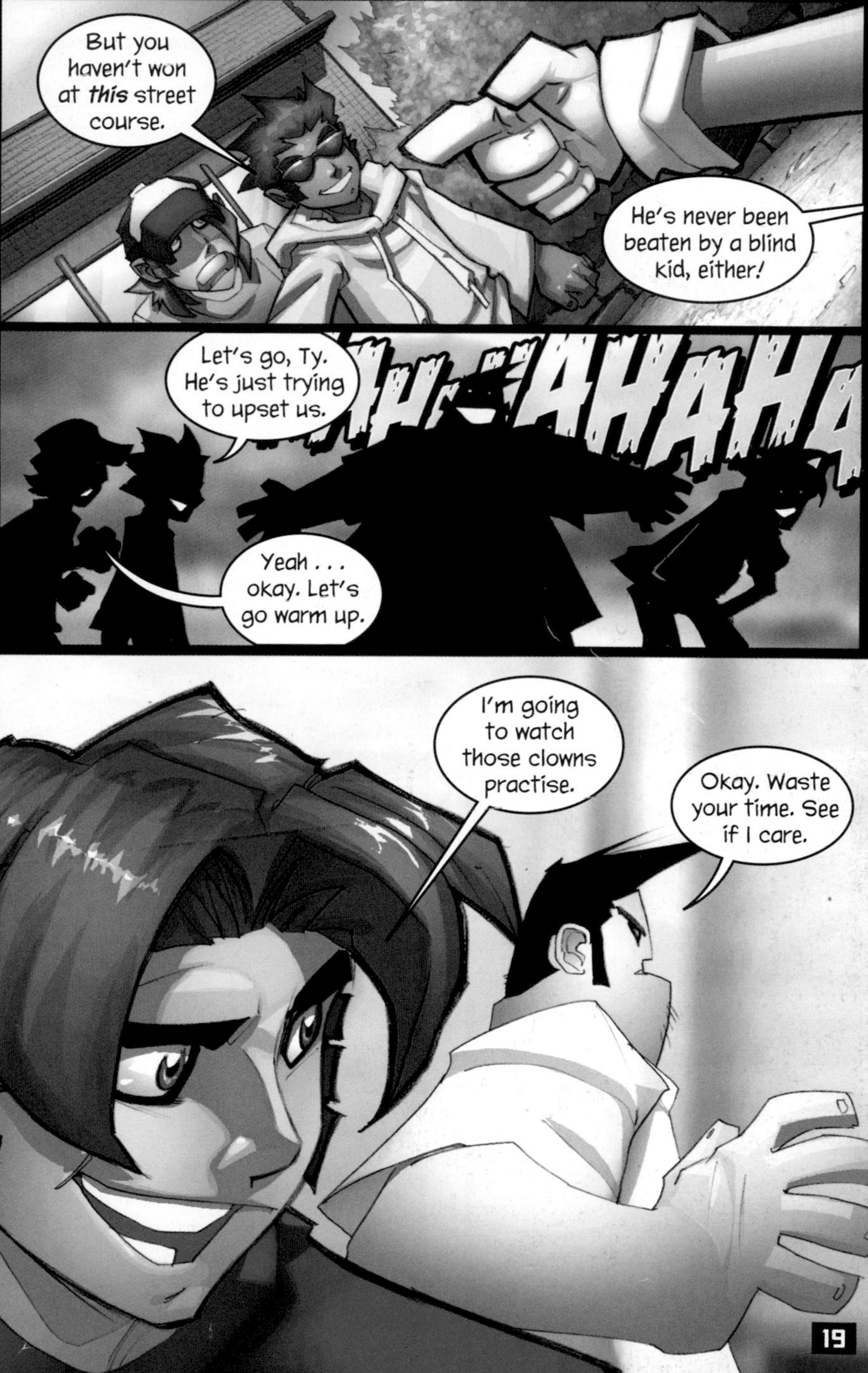
But you haven't won at *this* street course.
He's never been beaten by a blind kid, either!
Let's go, Ty. He's just trying to upset us.
AHAHA
Yeah . . . okay. Let's go warm up.
I'm going to watch those clowns practise.
Okay. Waste your time. See if I care.

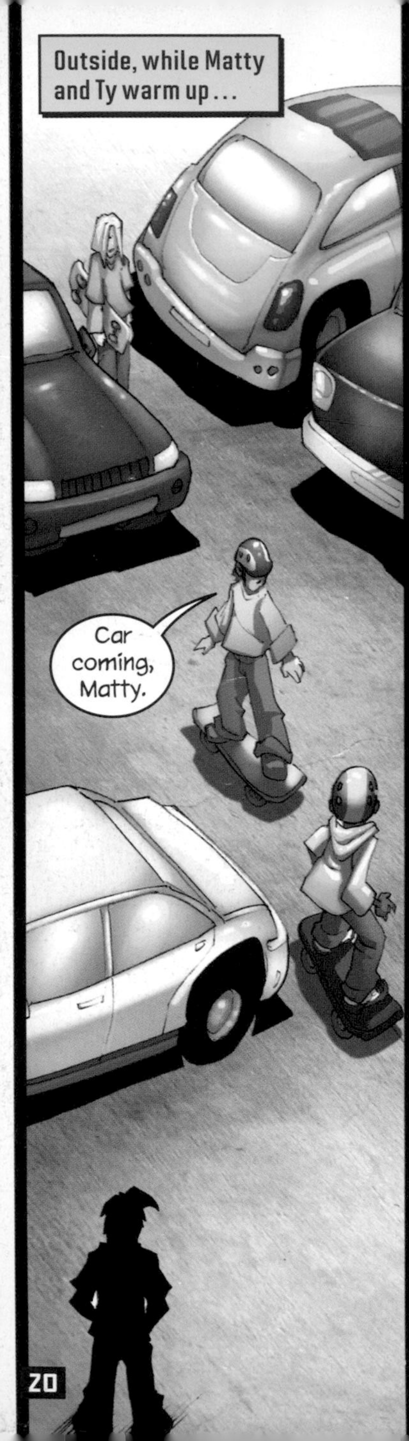
Outside, while Matty and Ty warm up . . .
Car coming, Matty.

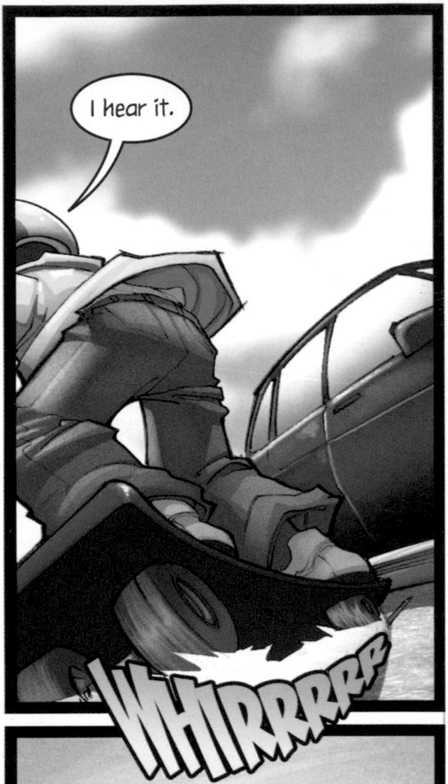
I hear it.
WHIRRRRR

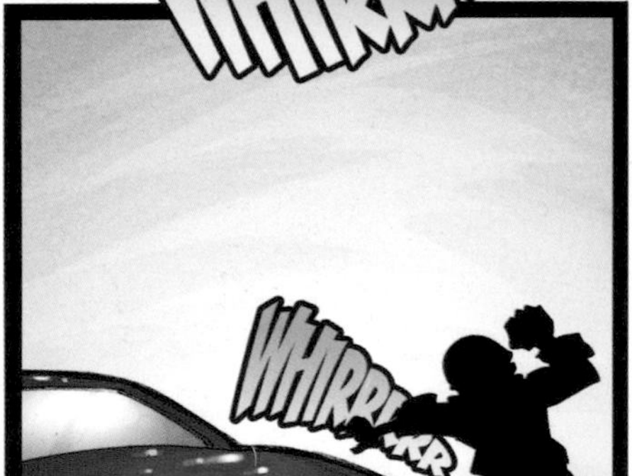
BF-981

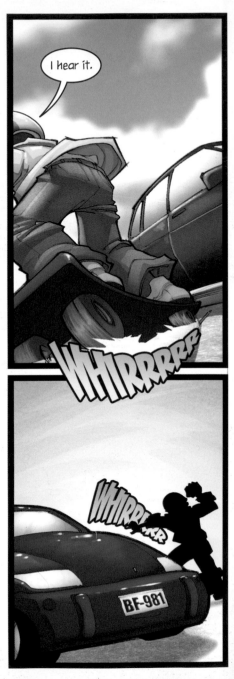

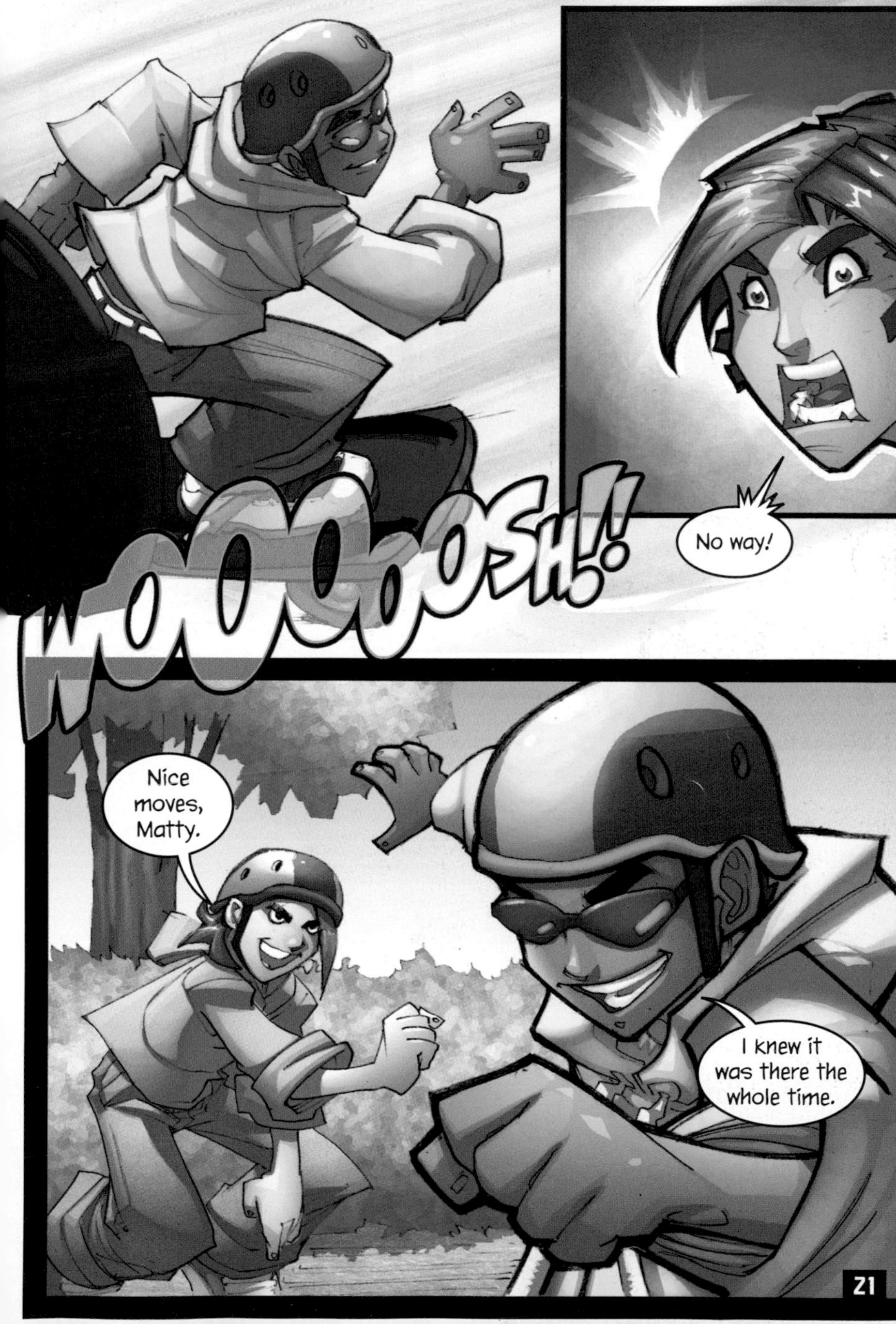
No way!
WOOOOOOSH!!
Nice moves, Matty.
I knew it was there the whole time.

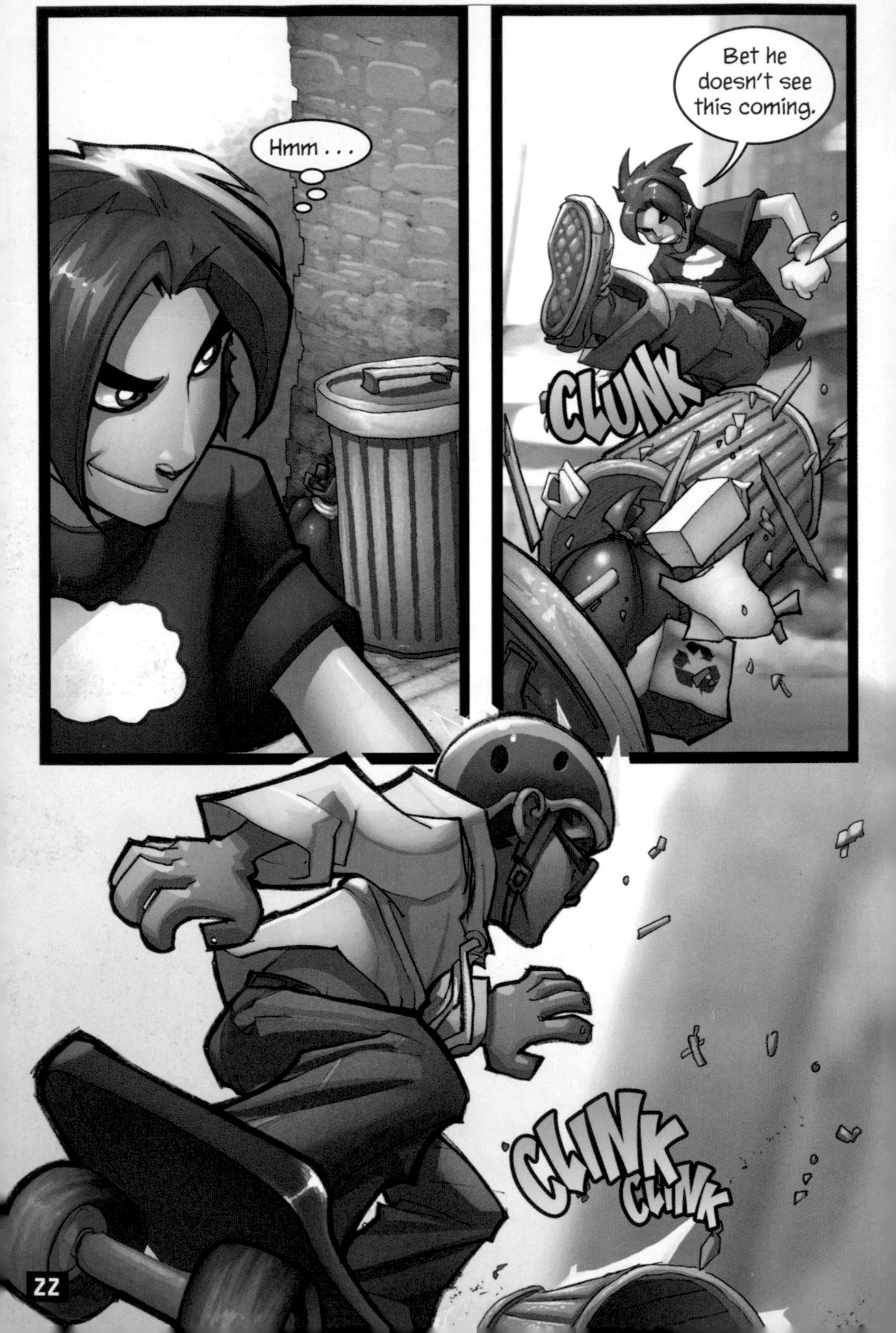
Hmm . . .
Bet he doesn't see this coming.
CLUNK
CLINK
CLINK

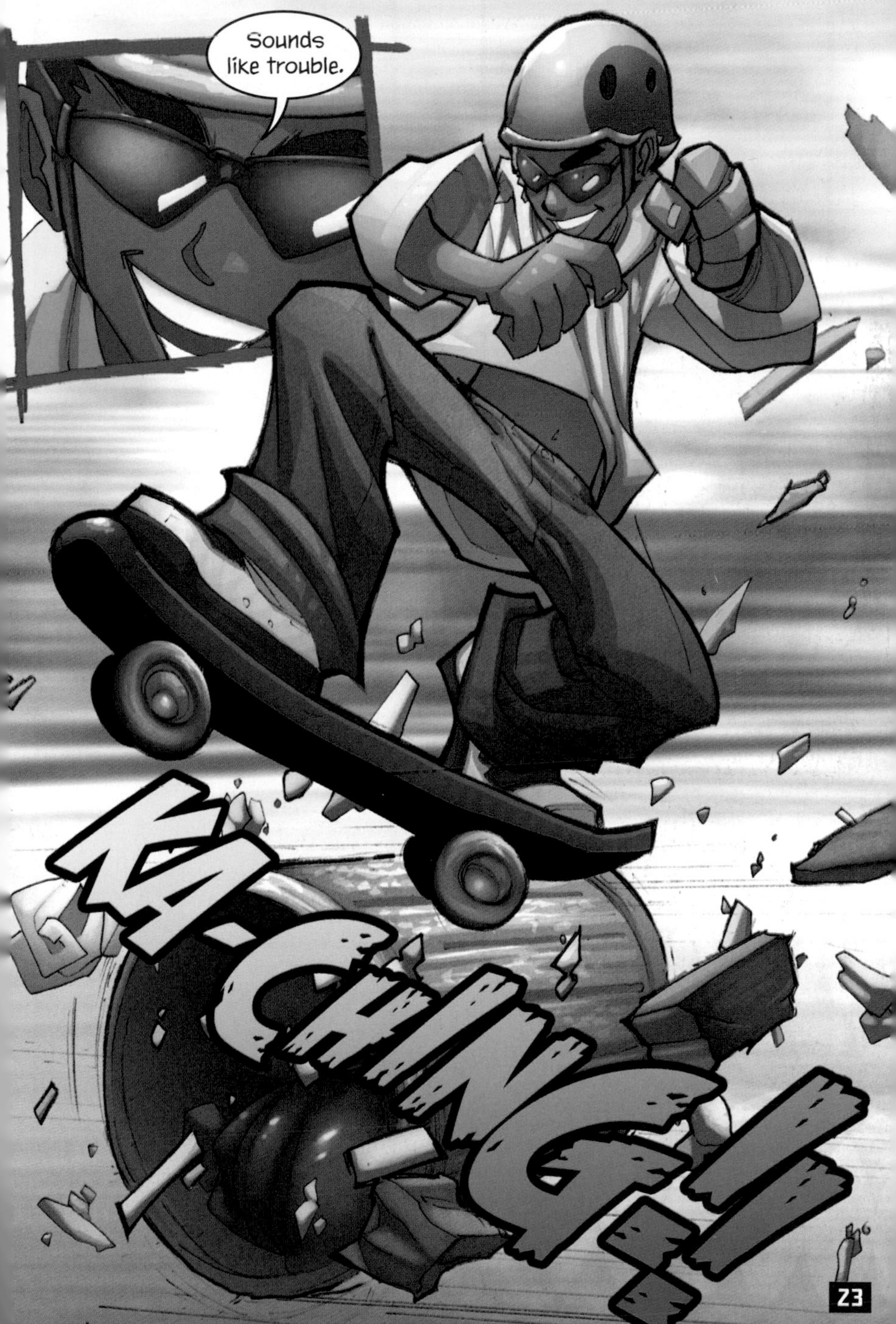
Sounds like trouble.
KA-CHING!!

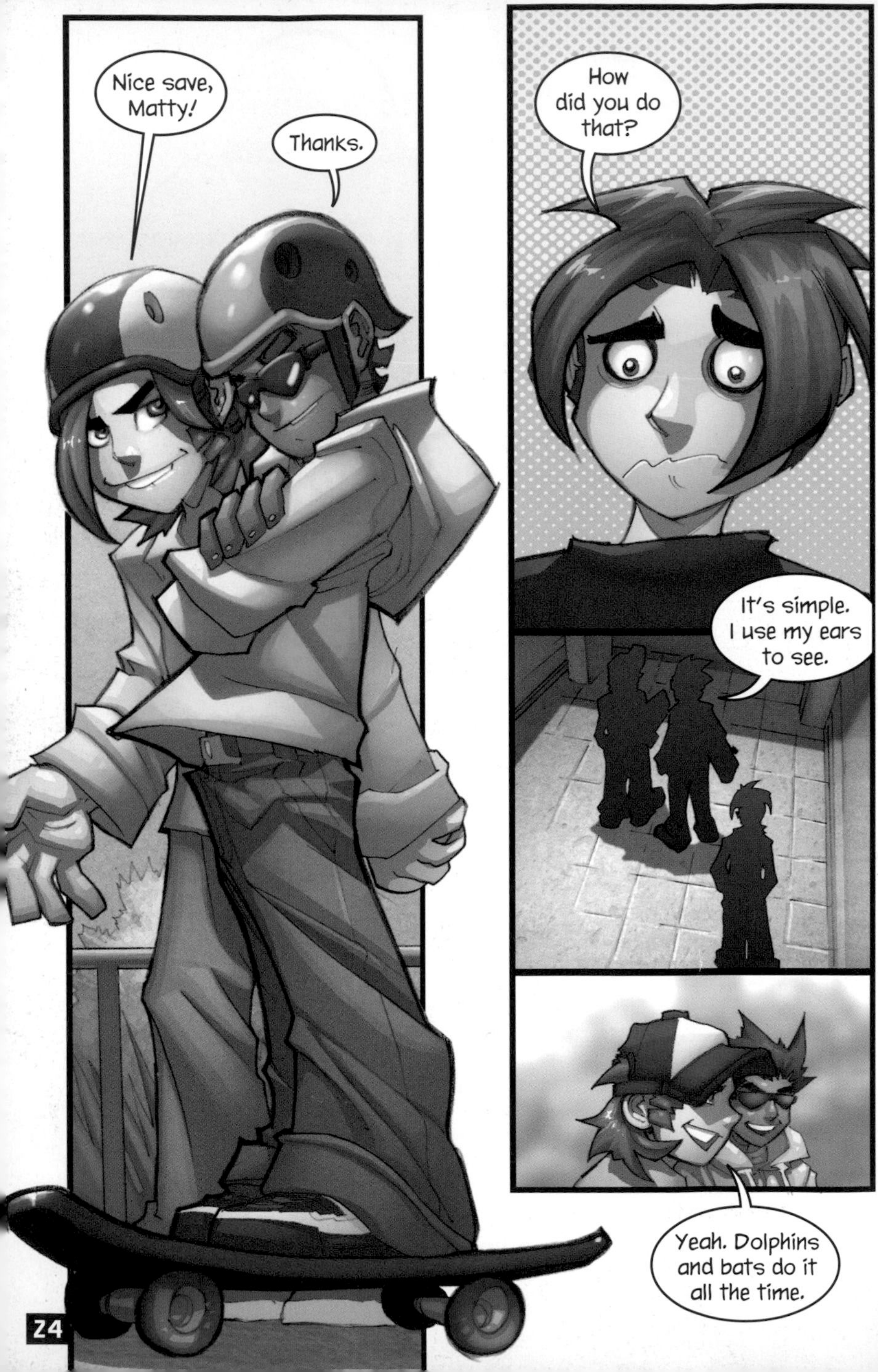
Nice save, Matty!
Thanks.
How did you do that?
It's simple. I use my ears to see.
Yeah. Dolphins and bats do it all the time.

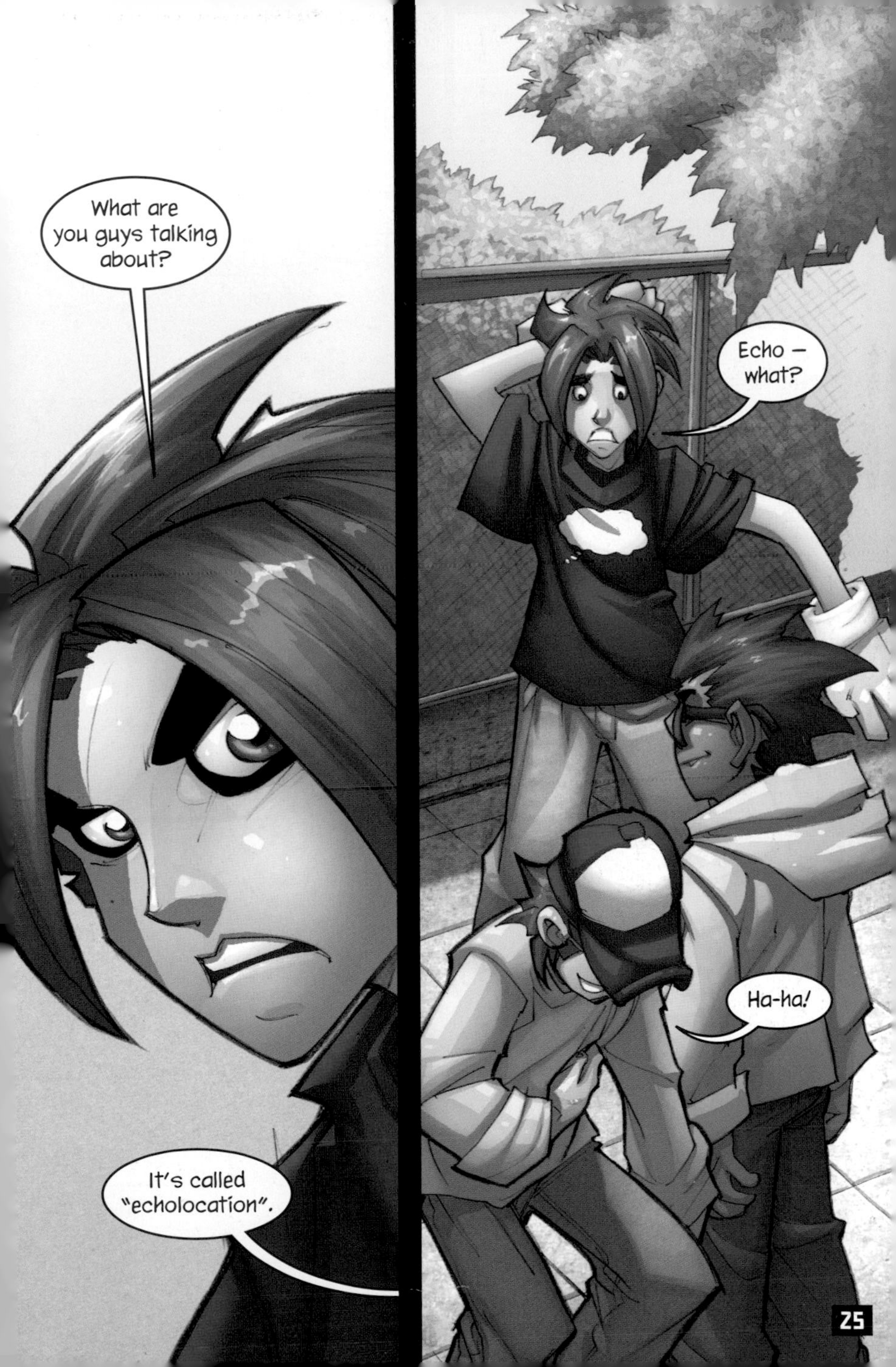
What are you guys talking about?
It's called "echolocation".
Echo — what?
Ha-ha!

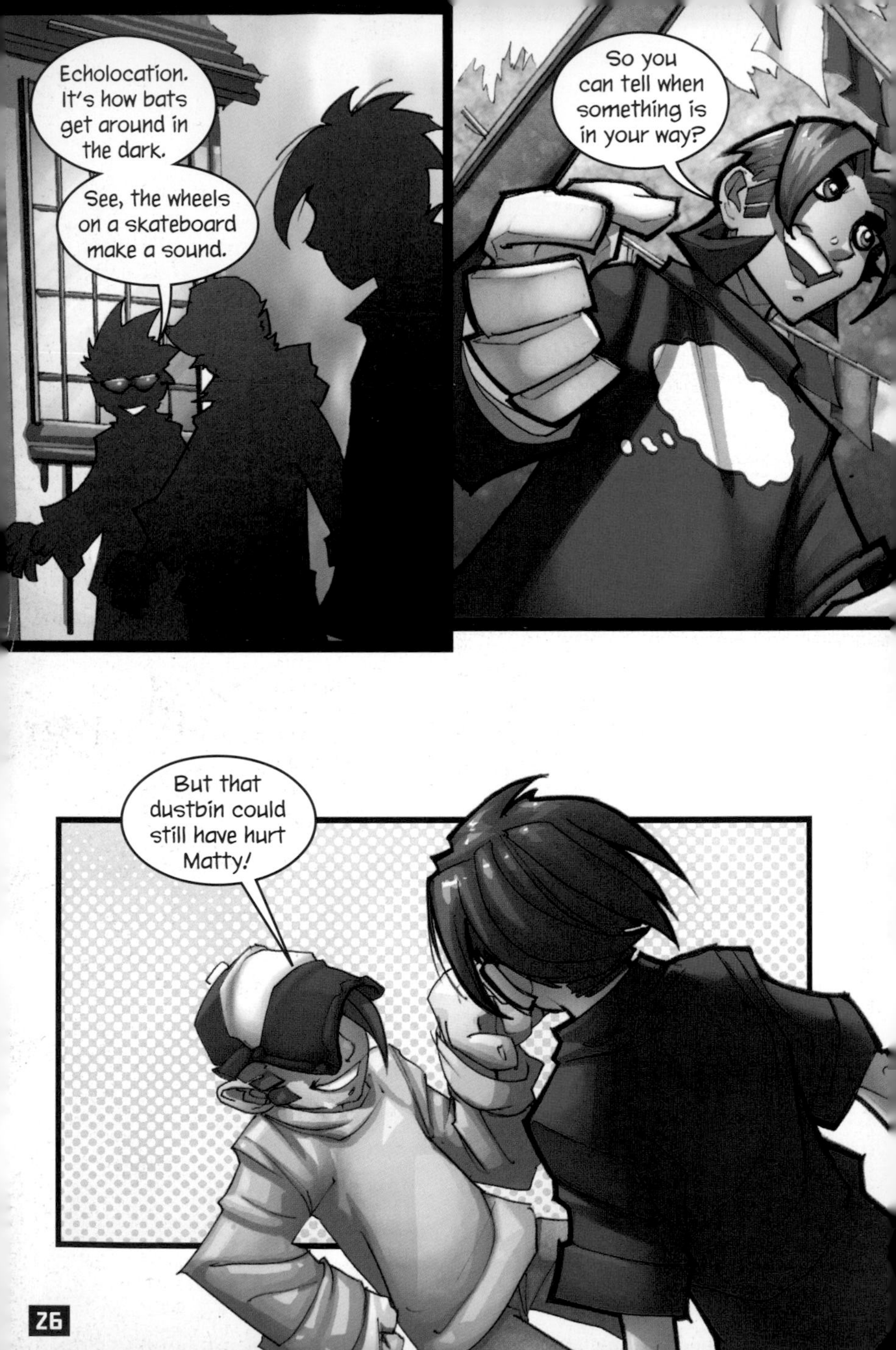
Echolocation. It's how bats get around in the dark.
See, the wheels on a skateboard make a sound.
So you can tell when something is in your way?
But that dustbin could still have hurt Matty!

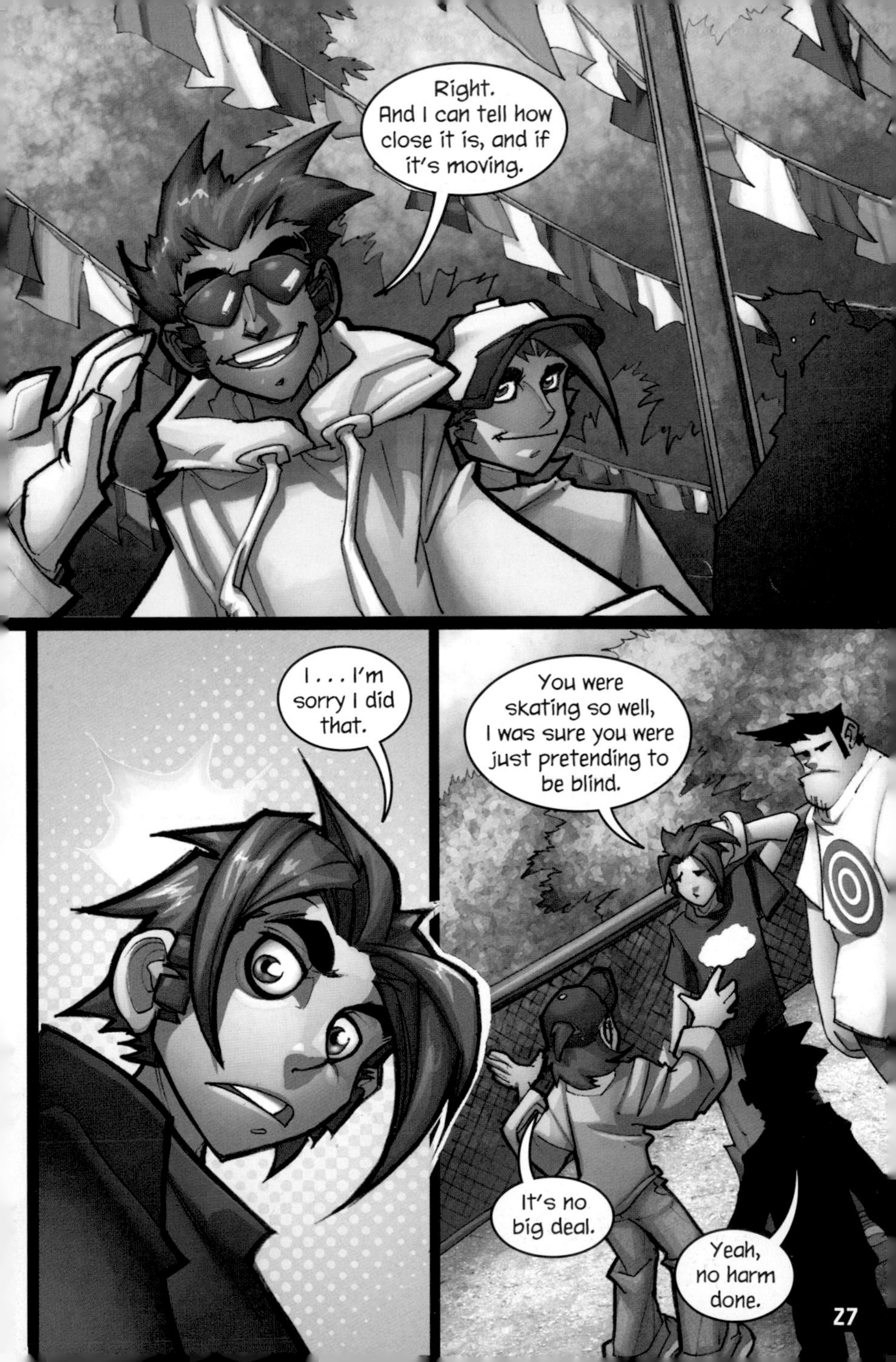
Right. And I can tell how close it is, and if it's moving.
I . . . I'm sorry I did that.
You were skating so well, I was sure you were just pretending to be blind.
It's no big deal.
Yeah, no harm done.

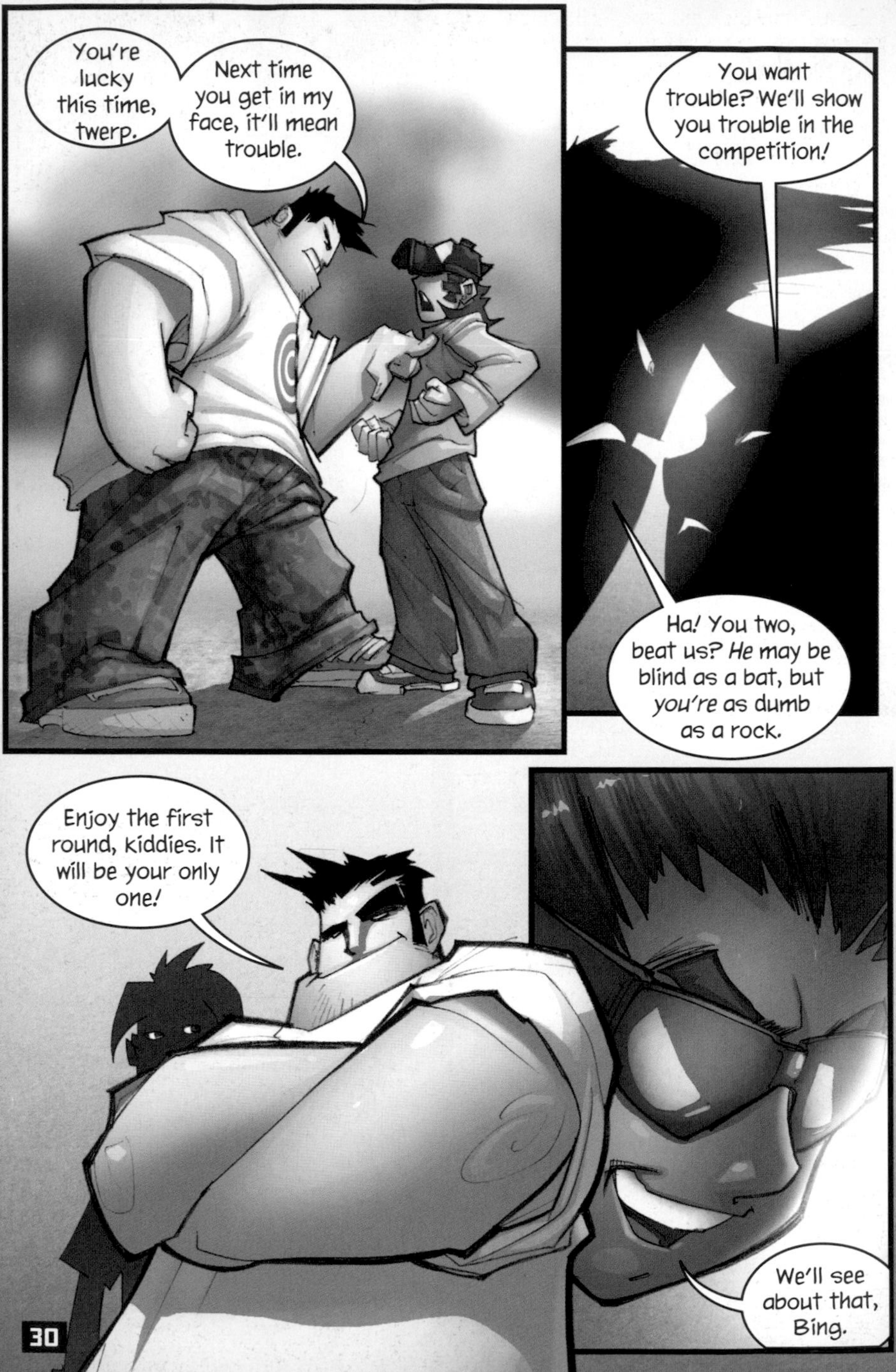
You're lucky this time, twerp.
Next time you get in my face, it'll mean trouble.
You want trouble? We'll show you trouble in the competition!
Ha! You two, beat us? *He* may be blind as a bat, but *you're* as dumb as a rock.
Enjoy the first round, kiddies. It will be your only one!
We'll see about that, Bing.

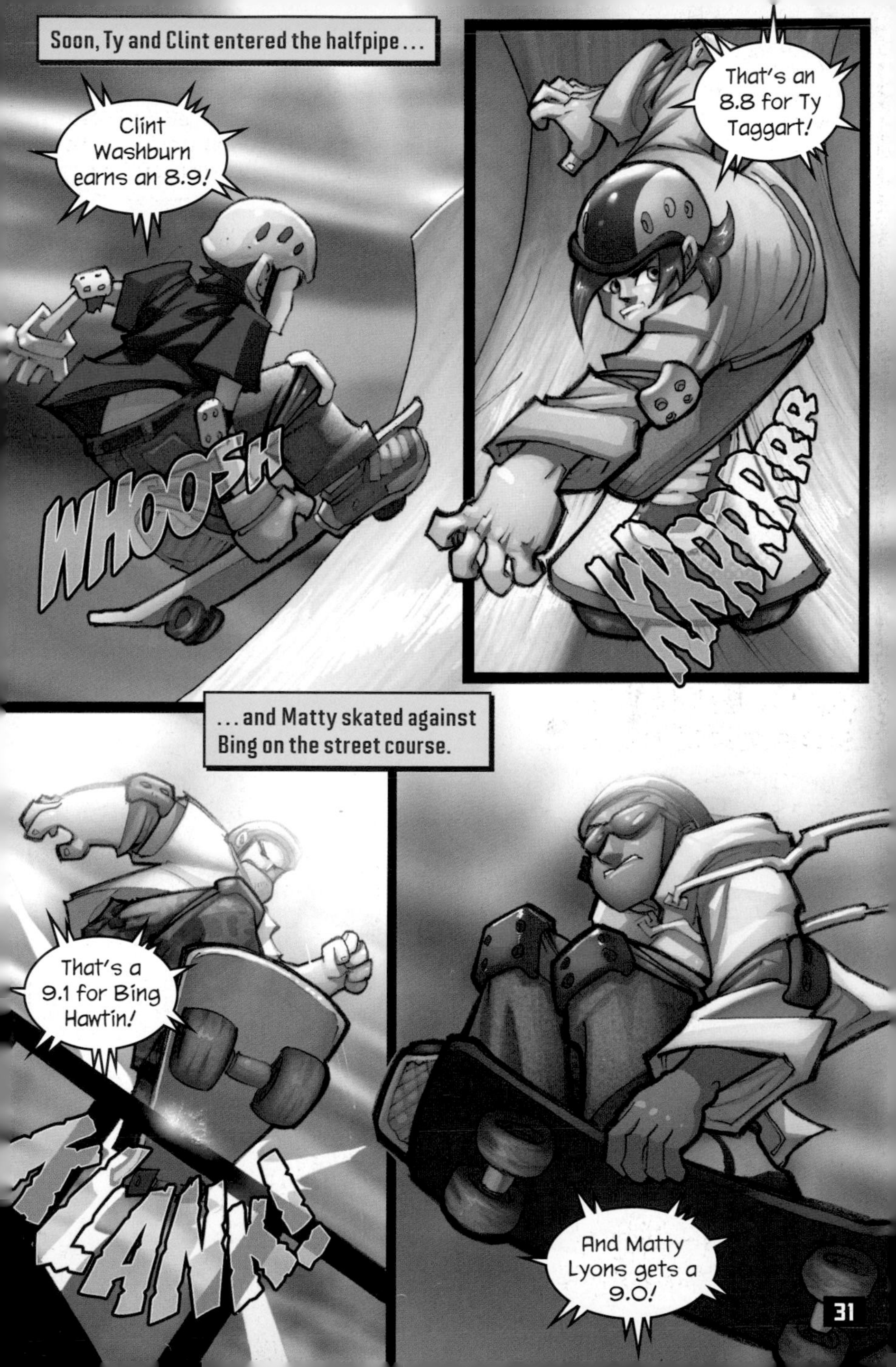

Soon, Ty and Clint entered the halfpipe . . .
Clint Washburn earns an 8.9!
WHOOSH
That's an 8.8 for Ty Taggart!
WHRRRR
. . . and Matty skated against Bing on the street course.
That's a 9.1 for Bing Hawtin!
FLANK!
And Matty Lyons gets a 9.0!

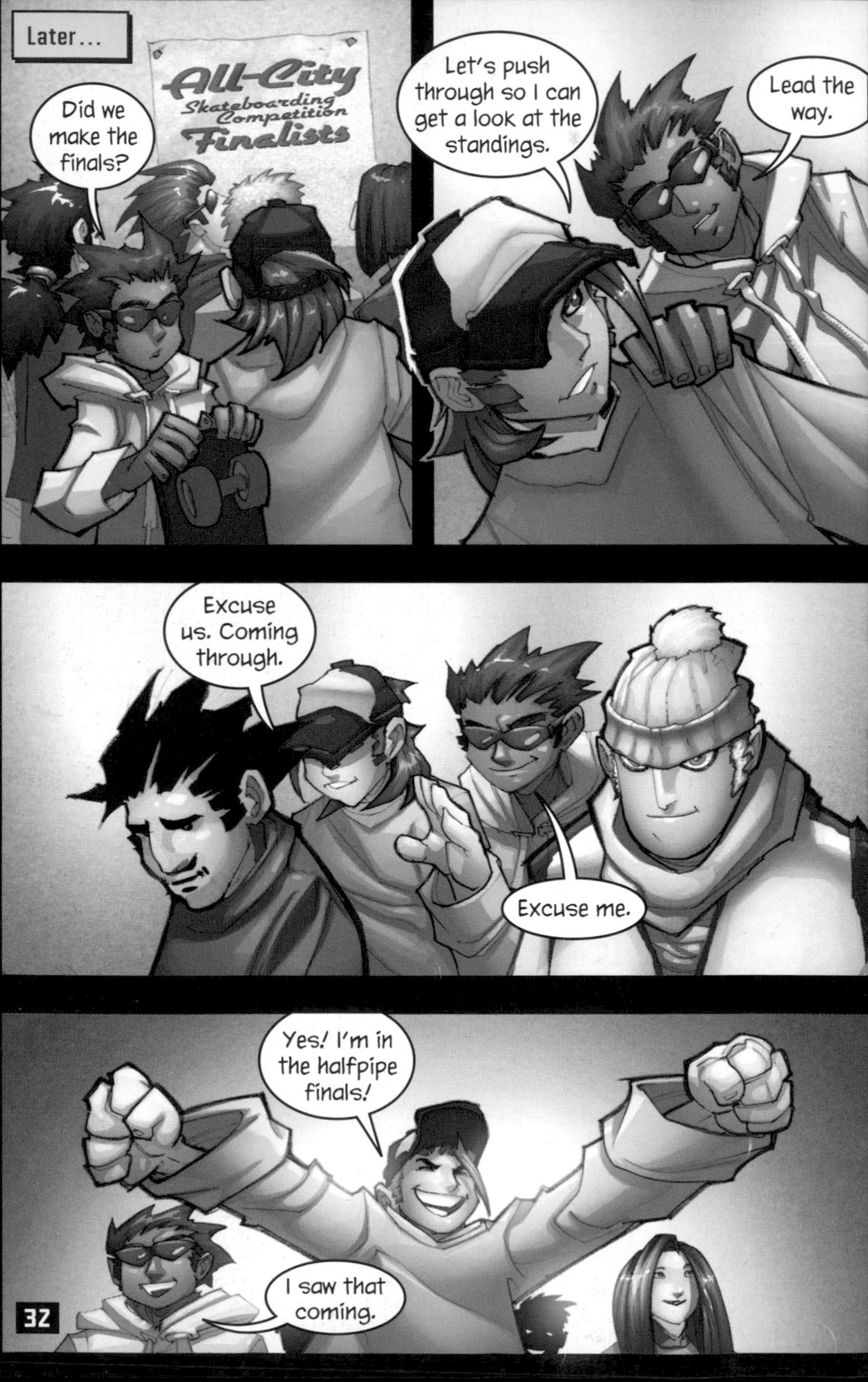

Later...
All-City Skateboarding Competition Finalists
Did we make the finals?
Let's push through so I can get a look at the standings.
Lead the way.
Excuse us. Coming through.
Excuse me.
Yes! I'm in the halfpipe finals!
I saw that coming.

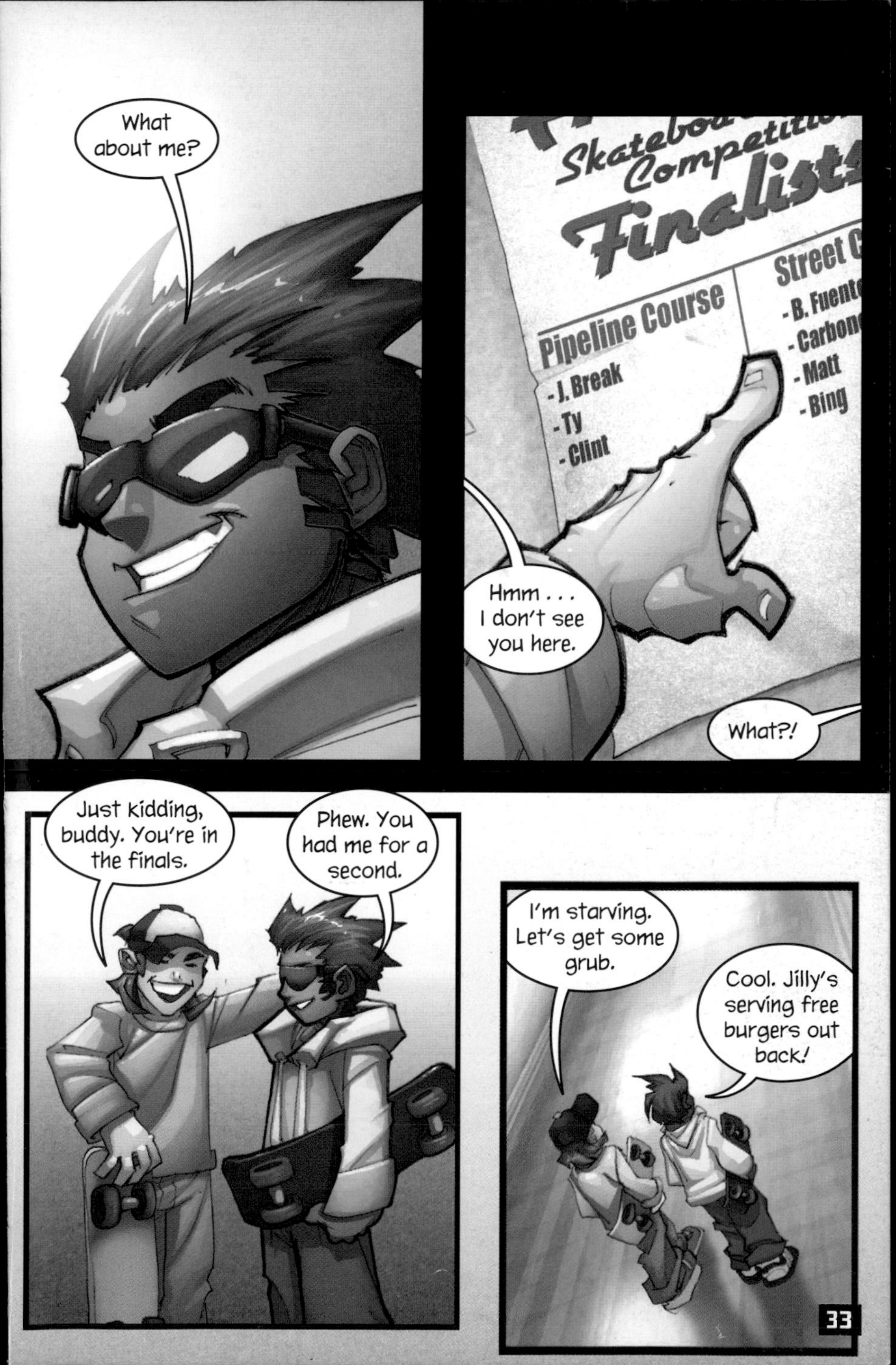
What about me?
Skateboard Competition Finalists
Pipeline Course
- J. Break
- Ty
- Clint
Street C
- B. Fuente
- Carbon
- Matt
- Bing
Hmm . . . I don't see you here.
What?!
Just kidding, buddy. You're in the finals.
Phew. You had me for a second.
I'm starving. Let's get some grub.
Cool. Jilly's serving free burgers out back!

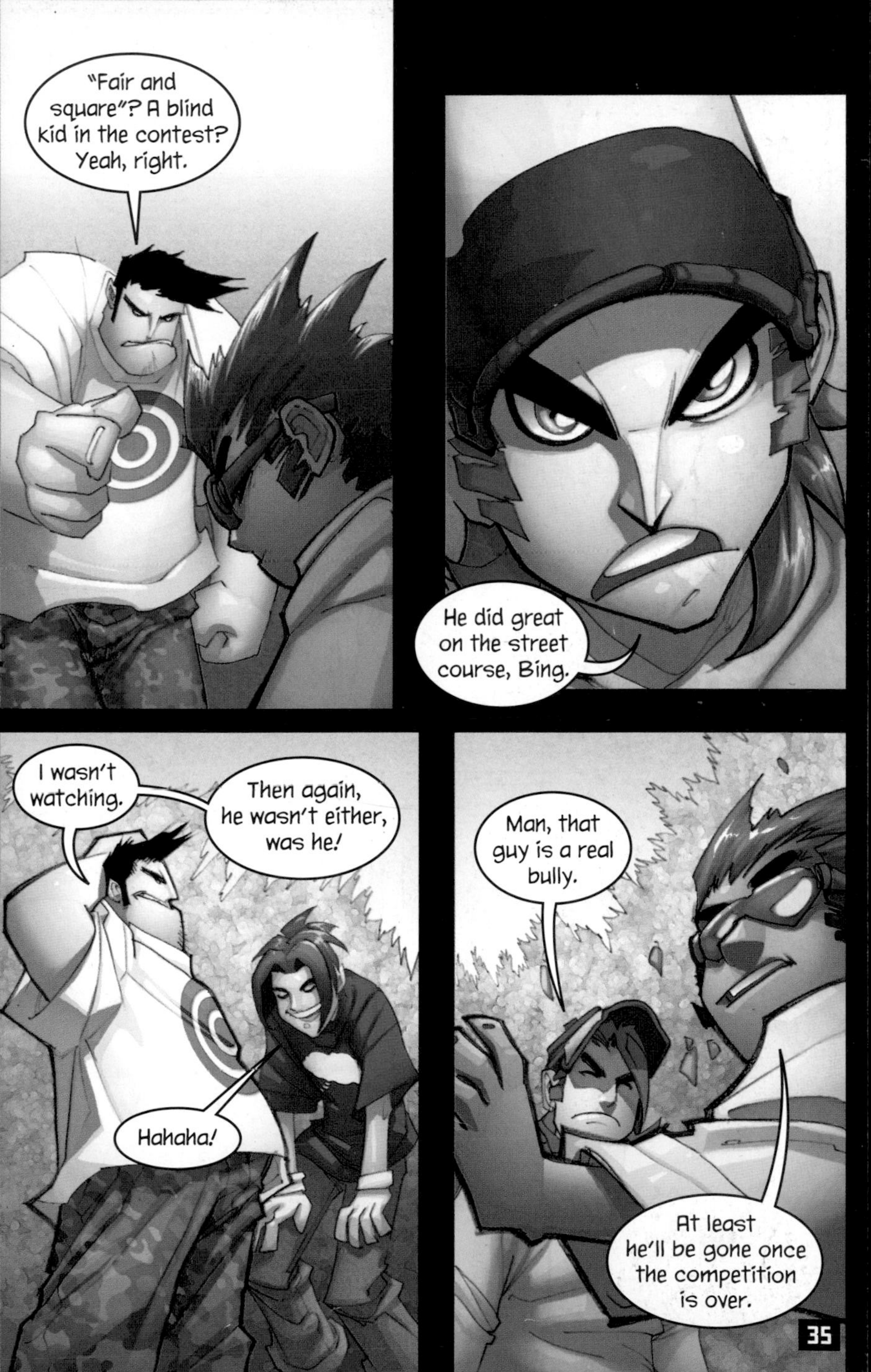
"Fair and square"? A blind kid in the contest? Yeah, right.
He did great on the street course, Bing.
I wasn't watching.
Then again, he wasn't either, was he!
Hahaha!
Man, that guy is a real bully.
At least he'll be gone once the competition is over.

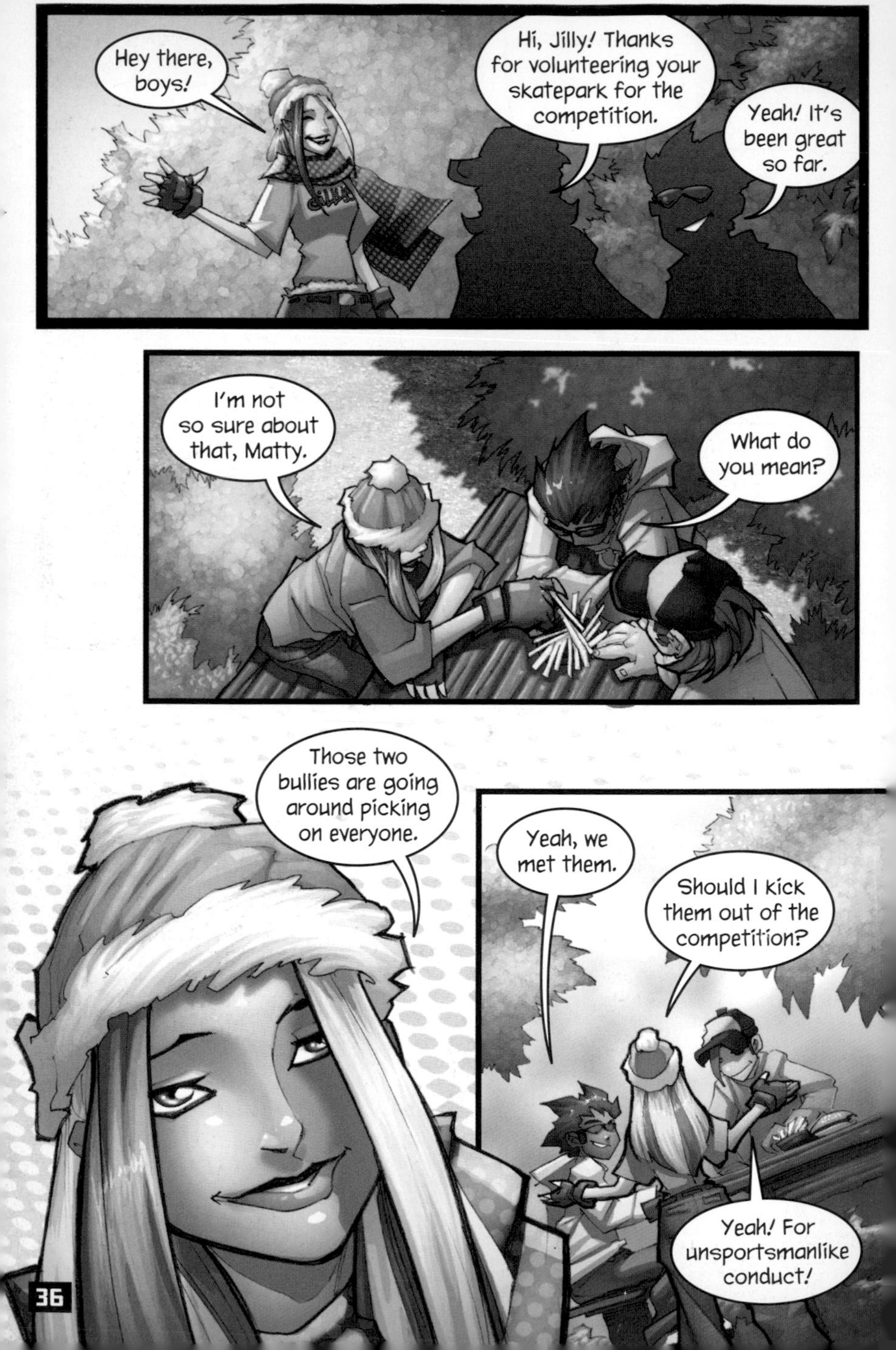
Hey there, boys!
Hi, Jilly! Thanks for volunteering your skatepark for the competition.
Yeah! It's been great so far.
I'm not so sure about that, Matty.
What do you mean?
Those two bullies are going around picking on everyone.
Yeah, we met them.
Should I kick them out of the competition?
Yeah! For unsportsmanlike conduct!

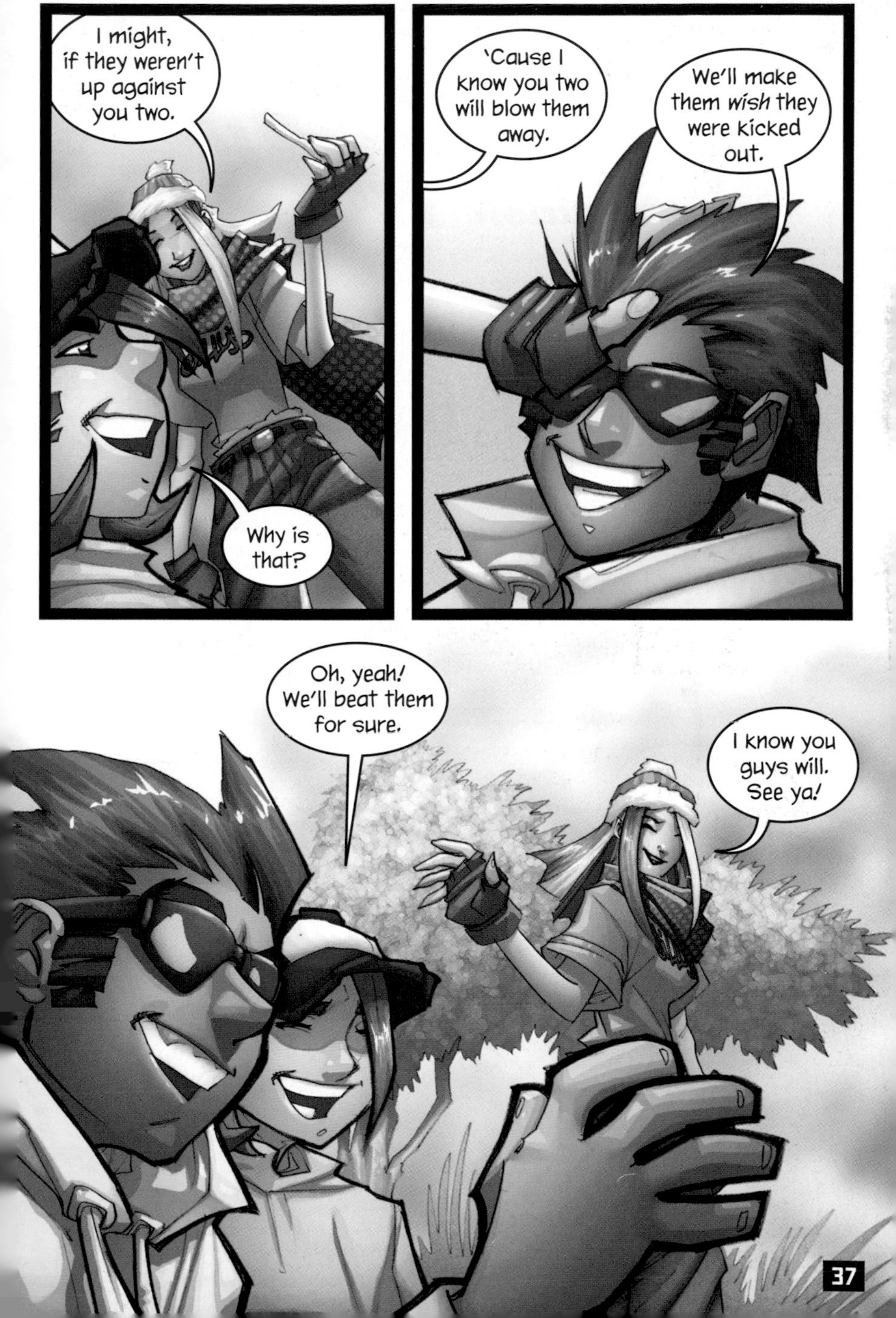
I might, if they weren't up against you two.
Why is that?
'Cause I know you two will blow them away.
We'll make them *wish* they were kicked out.
Oh, yeah! We'll beat them for sure.
I know you guys will. See ya!

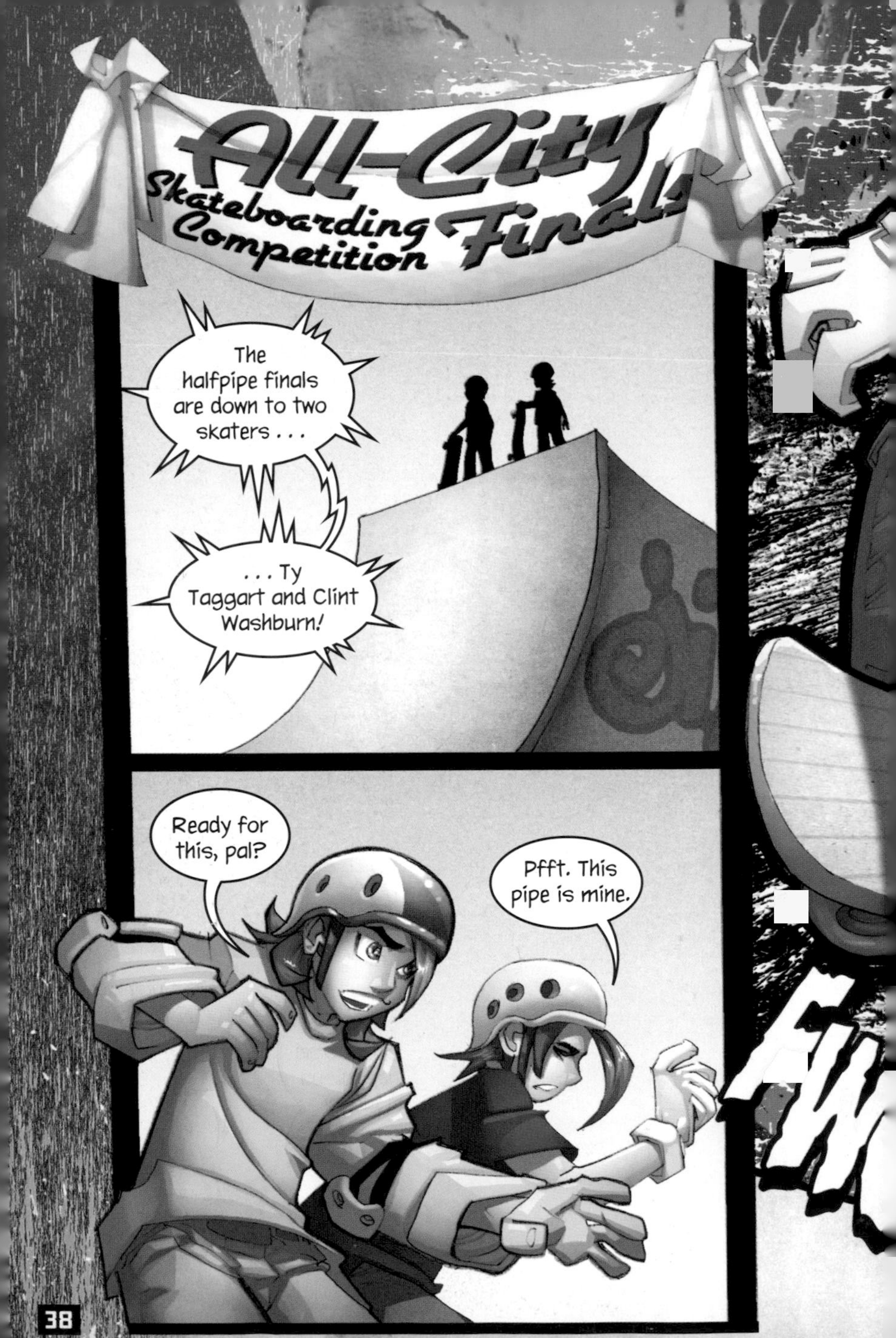
All-City Skateboarding Competition Finals
The halfpipe finals are down to two skaters . . .
. . . Ty Taggart and Clint Washburn!
Ready for this, pal?
Pfft. This pipe is mine.

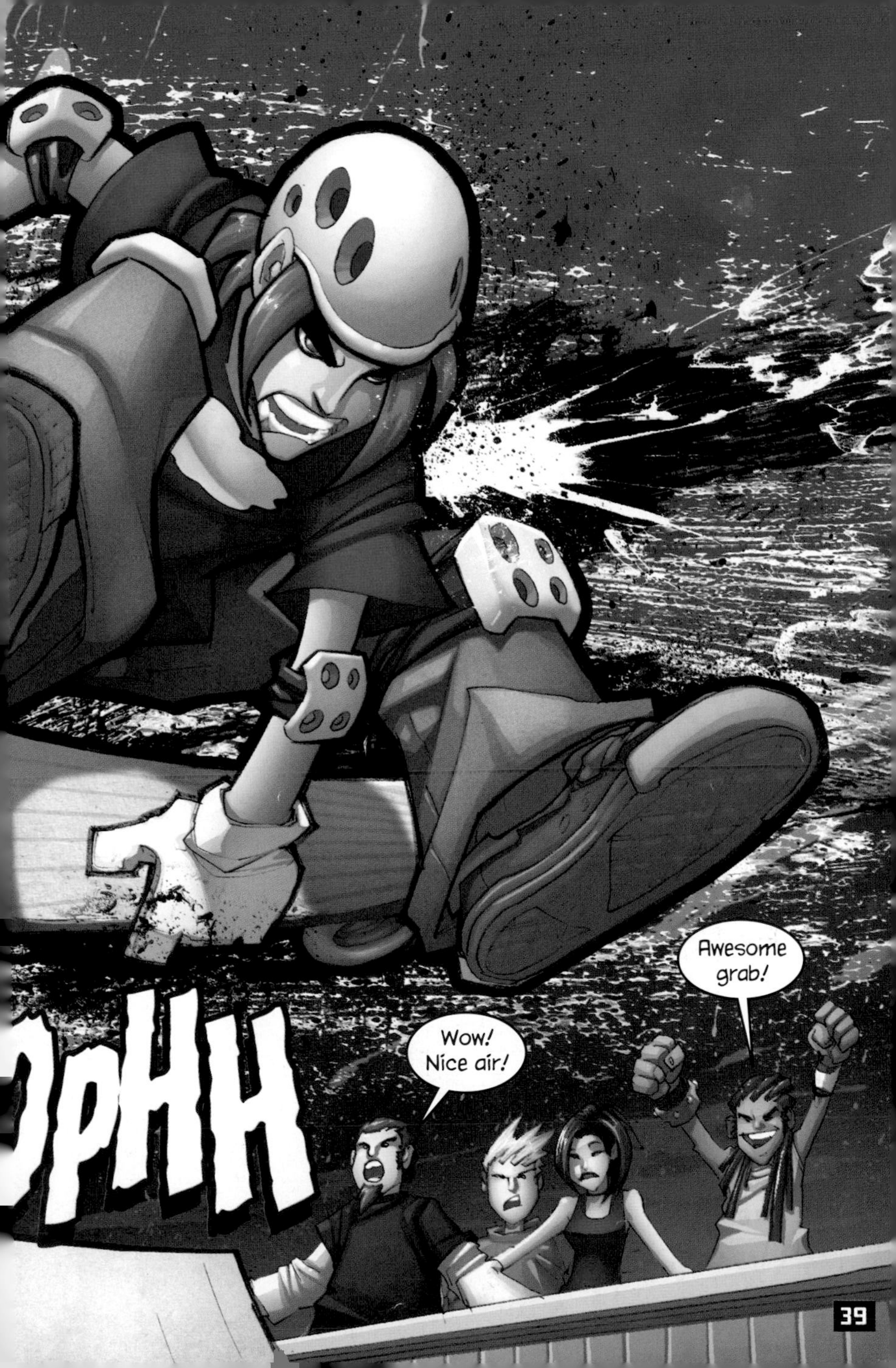
OPHH
Wow! Nice air!
Awesome grab!

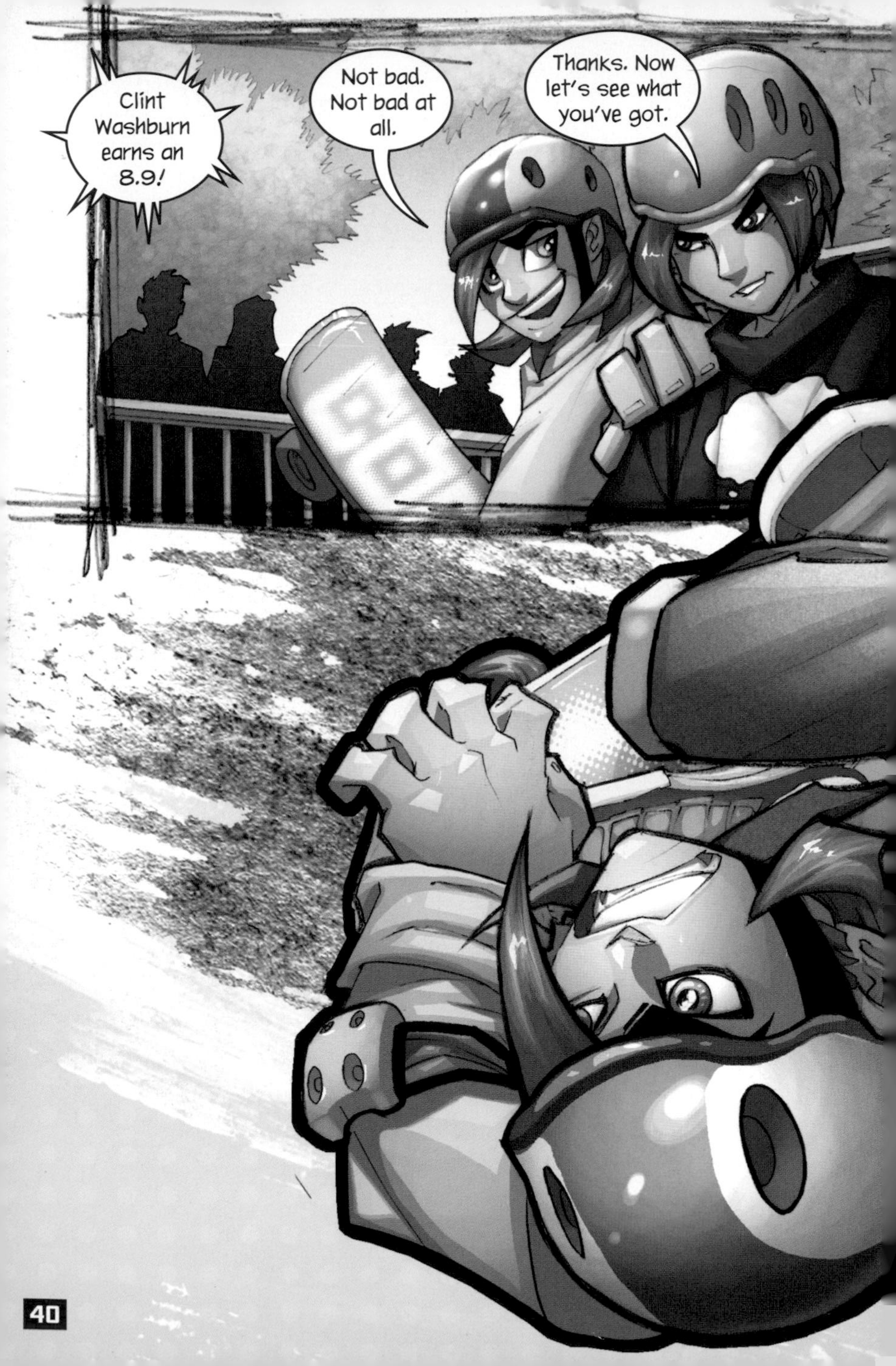

Clint Washburn earns an 8.9!
Not bad. Not bad at all.
Thanks. Now let's see what you've got.

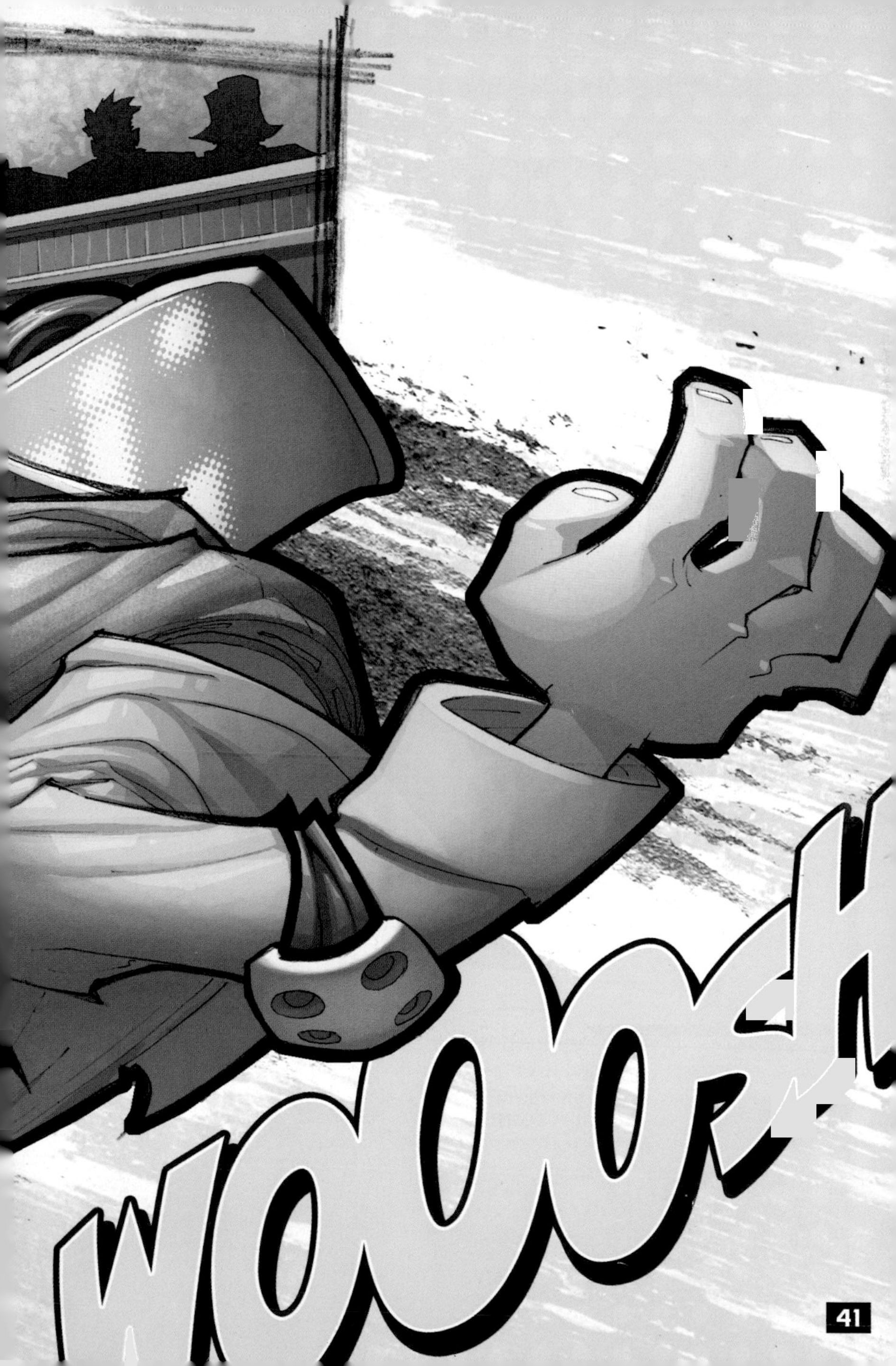
WOOOSH

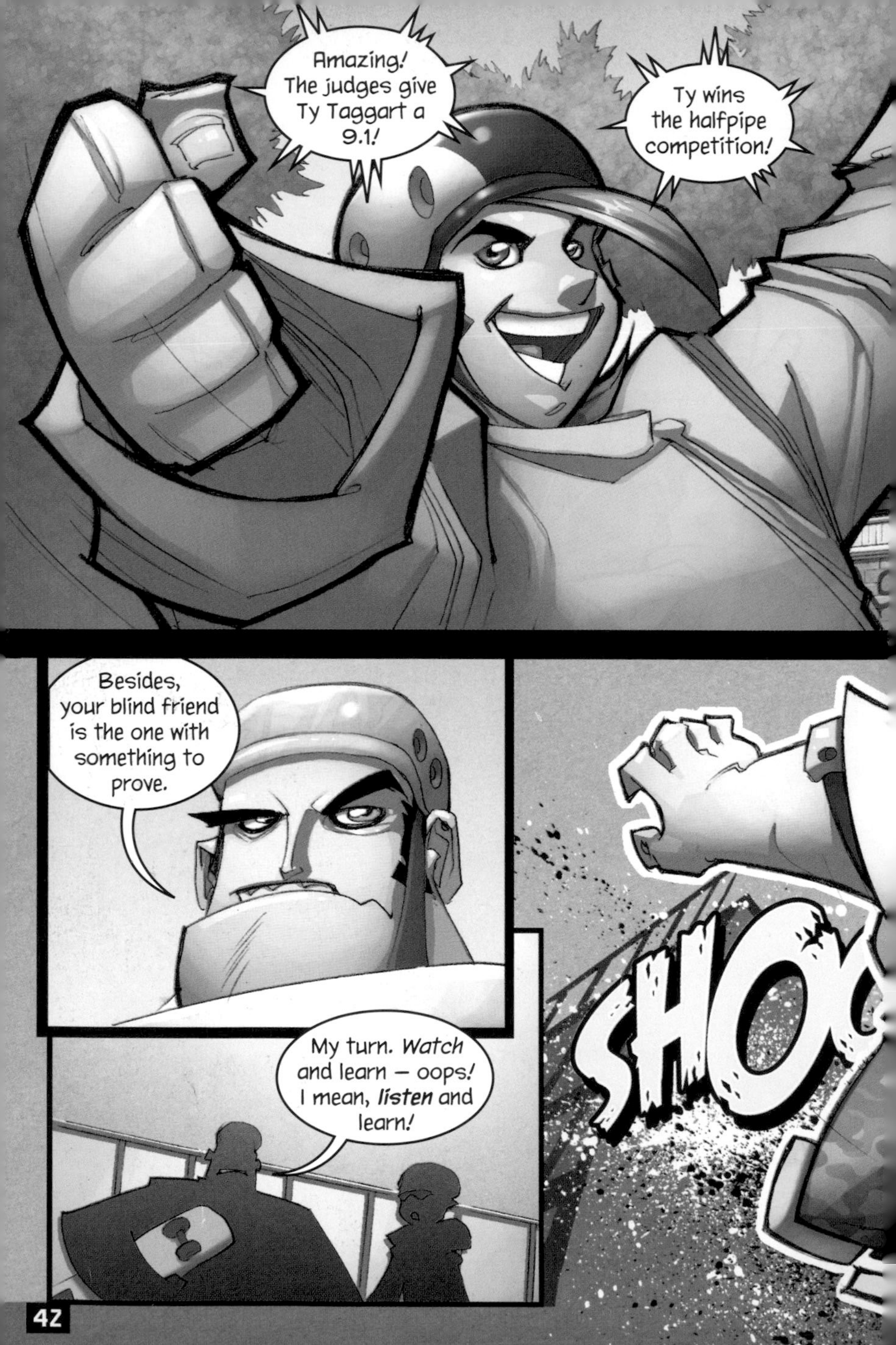
Amazing! The judges give Ty Taggart a 9.1!
Ty wins the halfpipe competition!
Besides, your blind friend is the one with something to prove.
My turn. *Watch* and learn – oops! I mean, ***listen*** and learn!
SHO

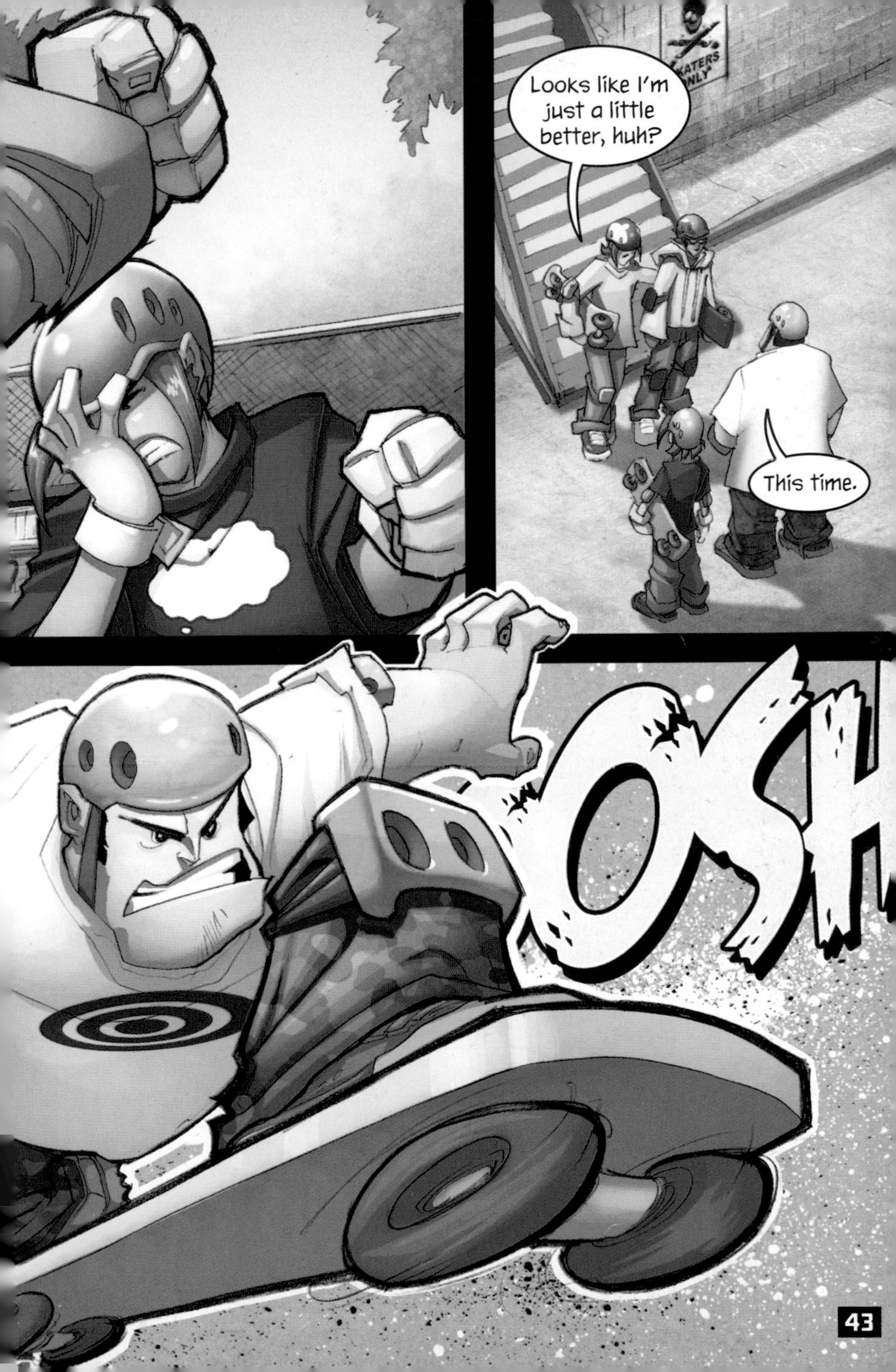
SKATERS ONLY
Looks like I'm just a little better, huh?
This time.
OSH

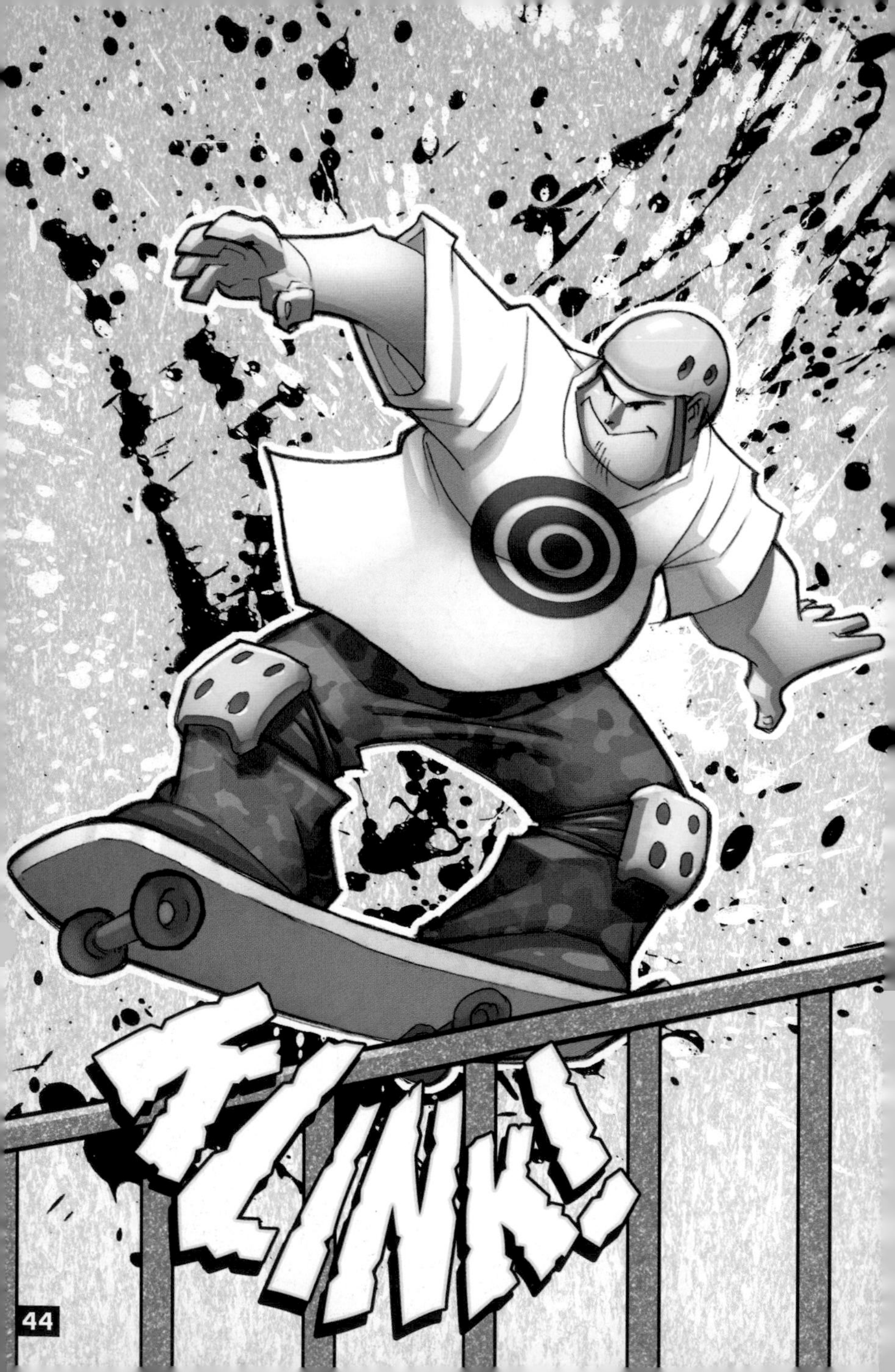
ZLINK!

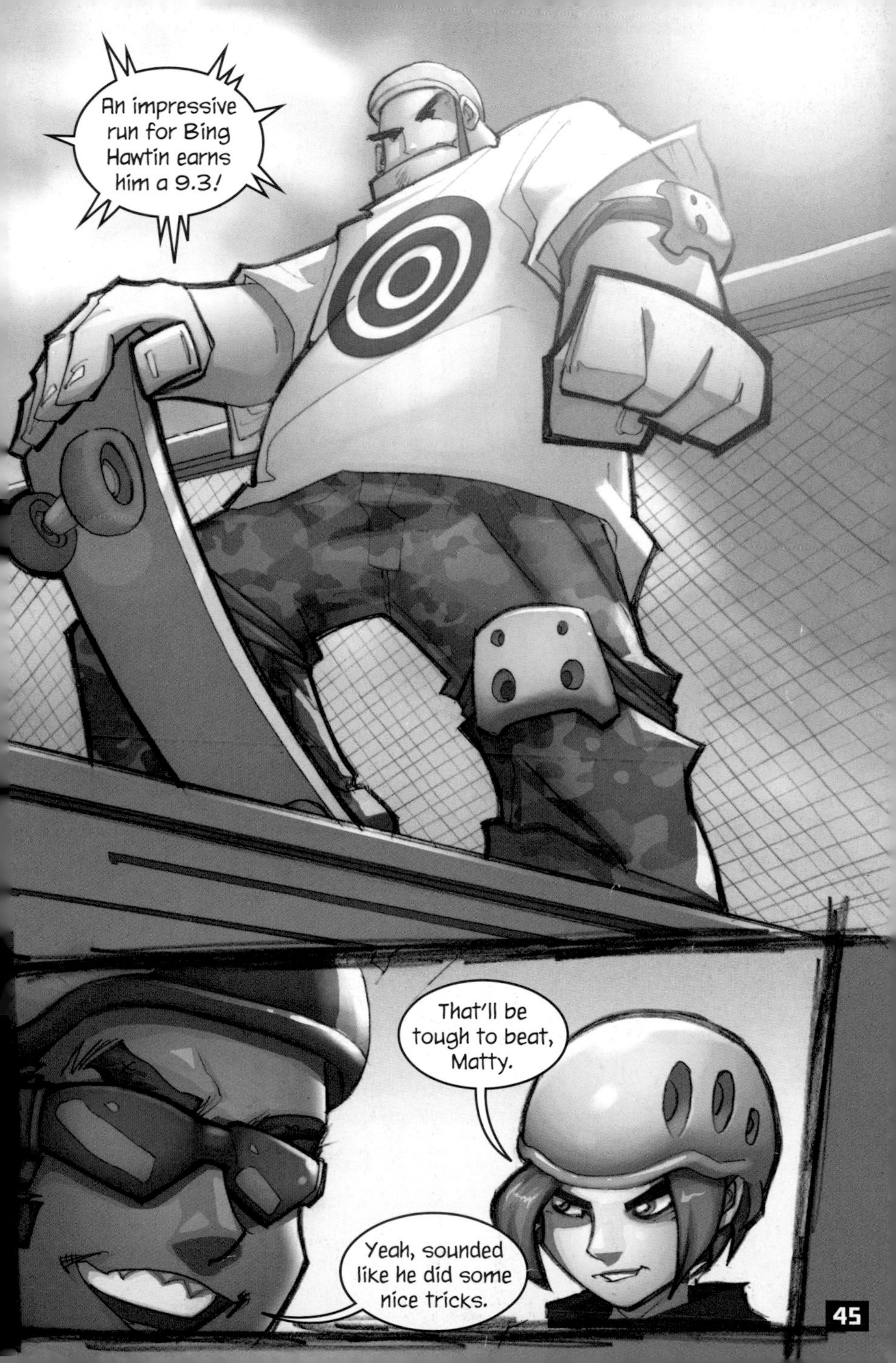
An impressive run for Bing Hawtin earns him a 9.3!
That'll be tough to beat, Matty.
Yeah, sounded like he did some nice tricks.

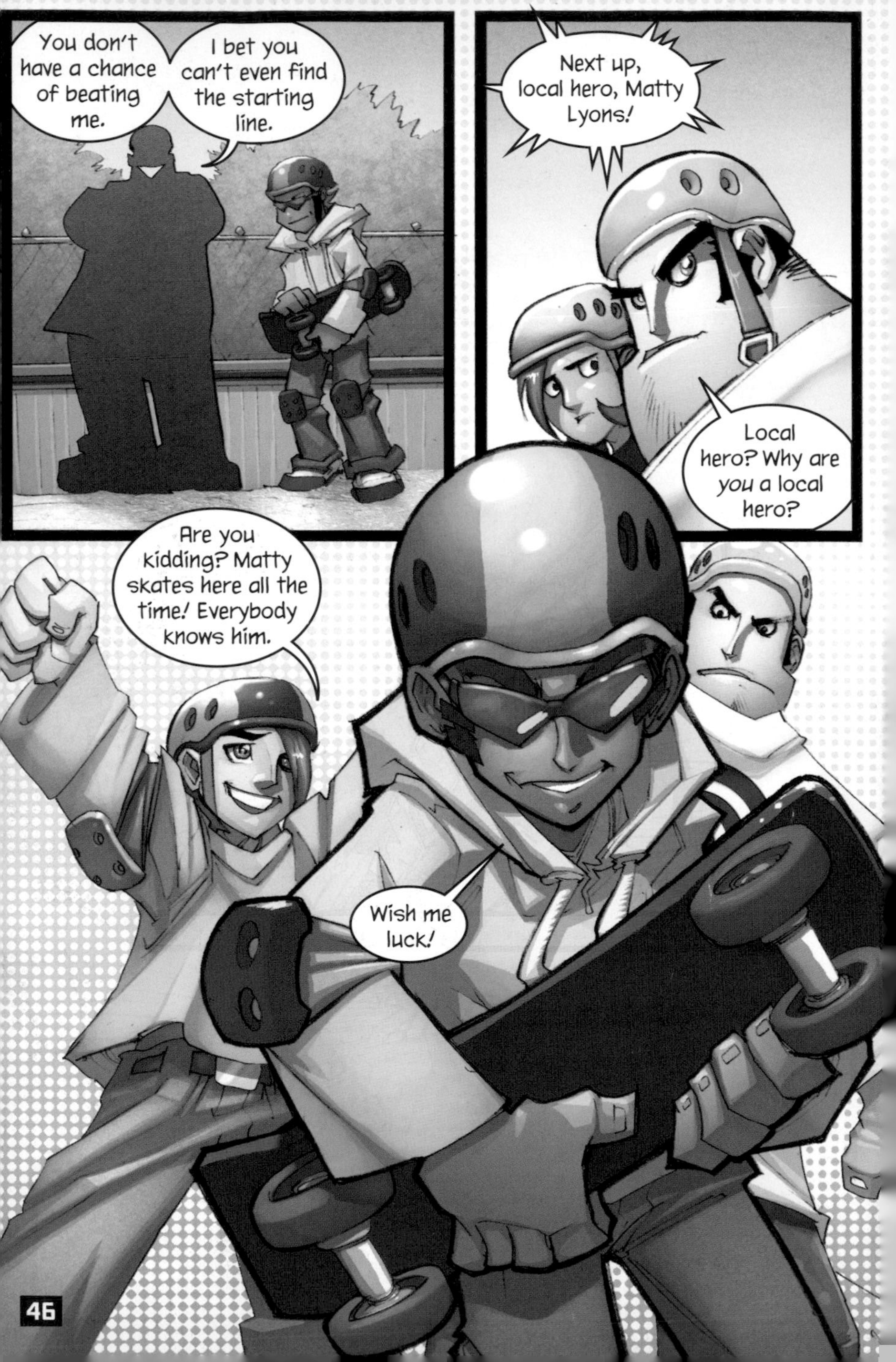
You don't have a chance of beating me.
I bet you can't even find the starting line.
Next up, local hero, Matty Lyons!
Local hero? Why are *you* a local hero?
Are you kidding? Matty skates here all the time! Everybody knows him.
Wish me luck!

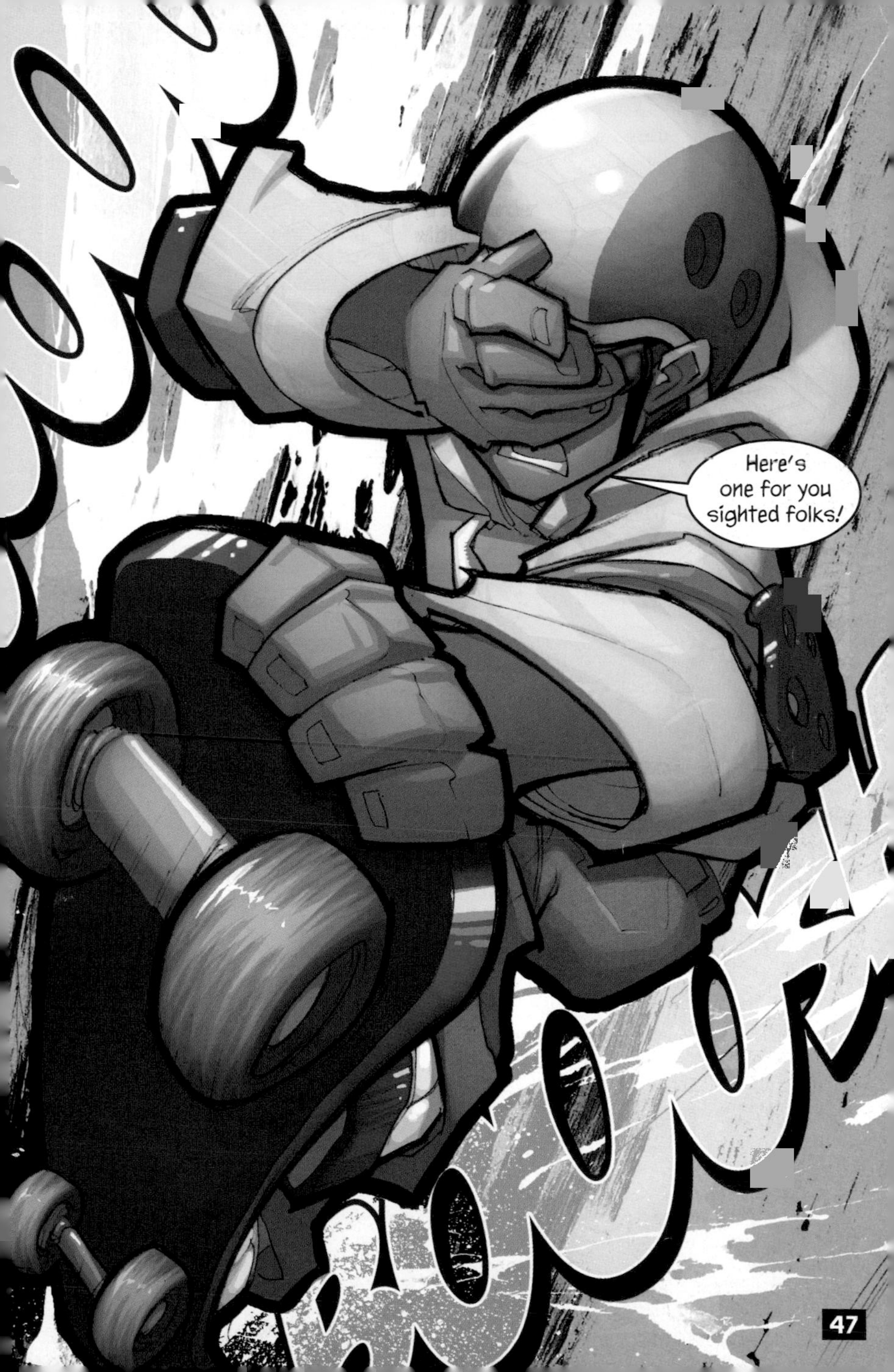
Here's one for you sighted folks!

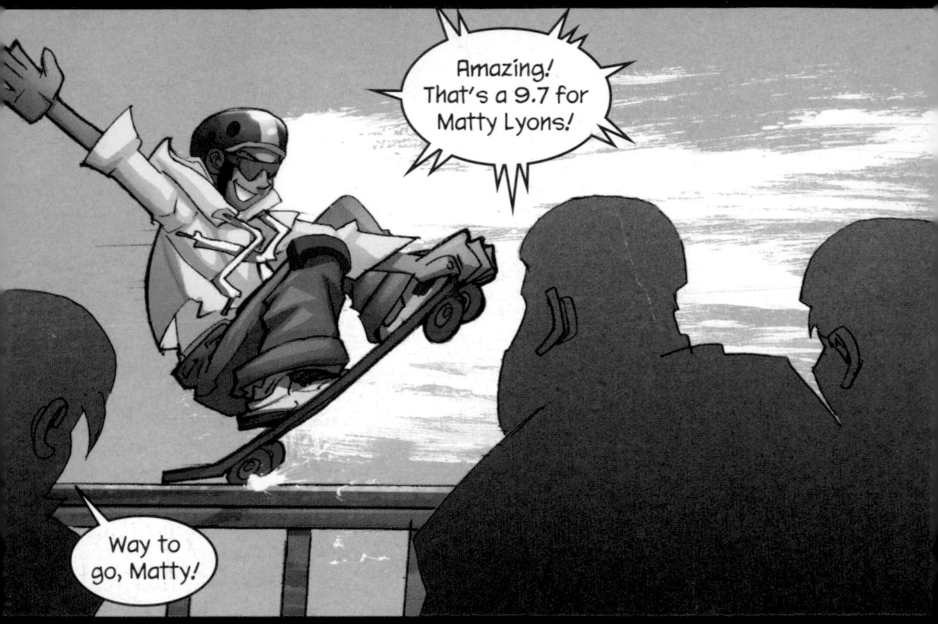
Amazing! That's a 9.7 for Matty Lyons!
Way to go, Matty!

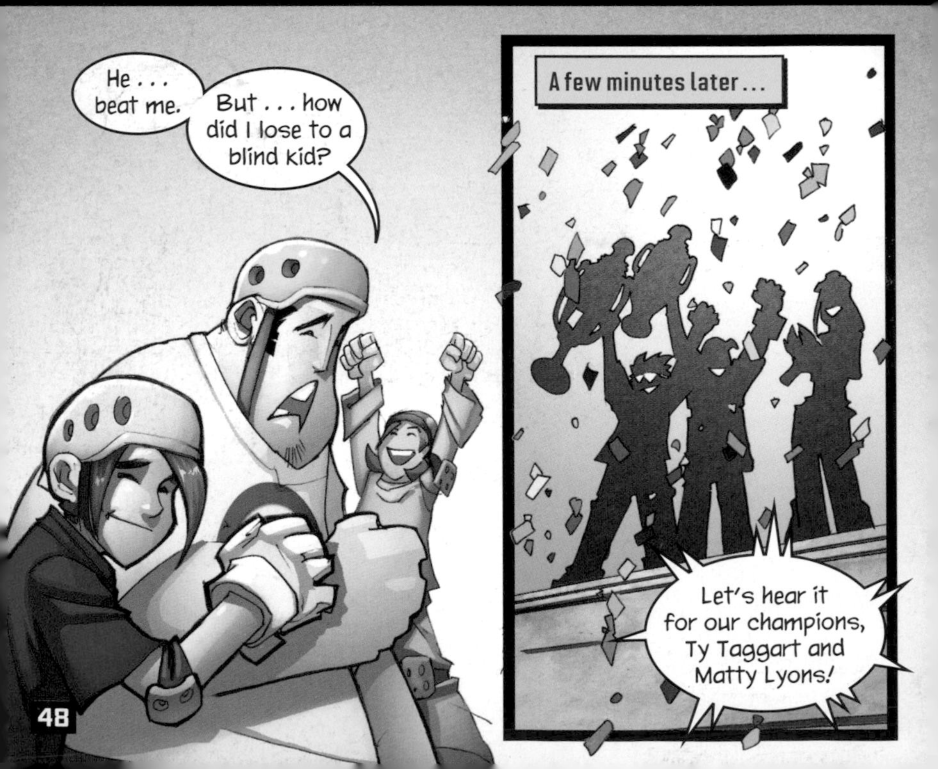
He . . . beat me.
But . . . how did I lose to a blind kid?
A few minutes later . . .
Let's hear it for our champions, Ty Taggart and Matty Lyons!

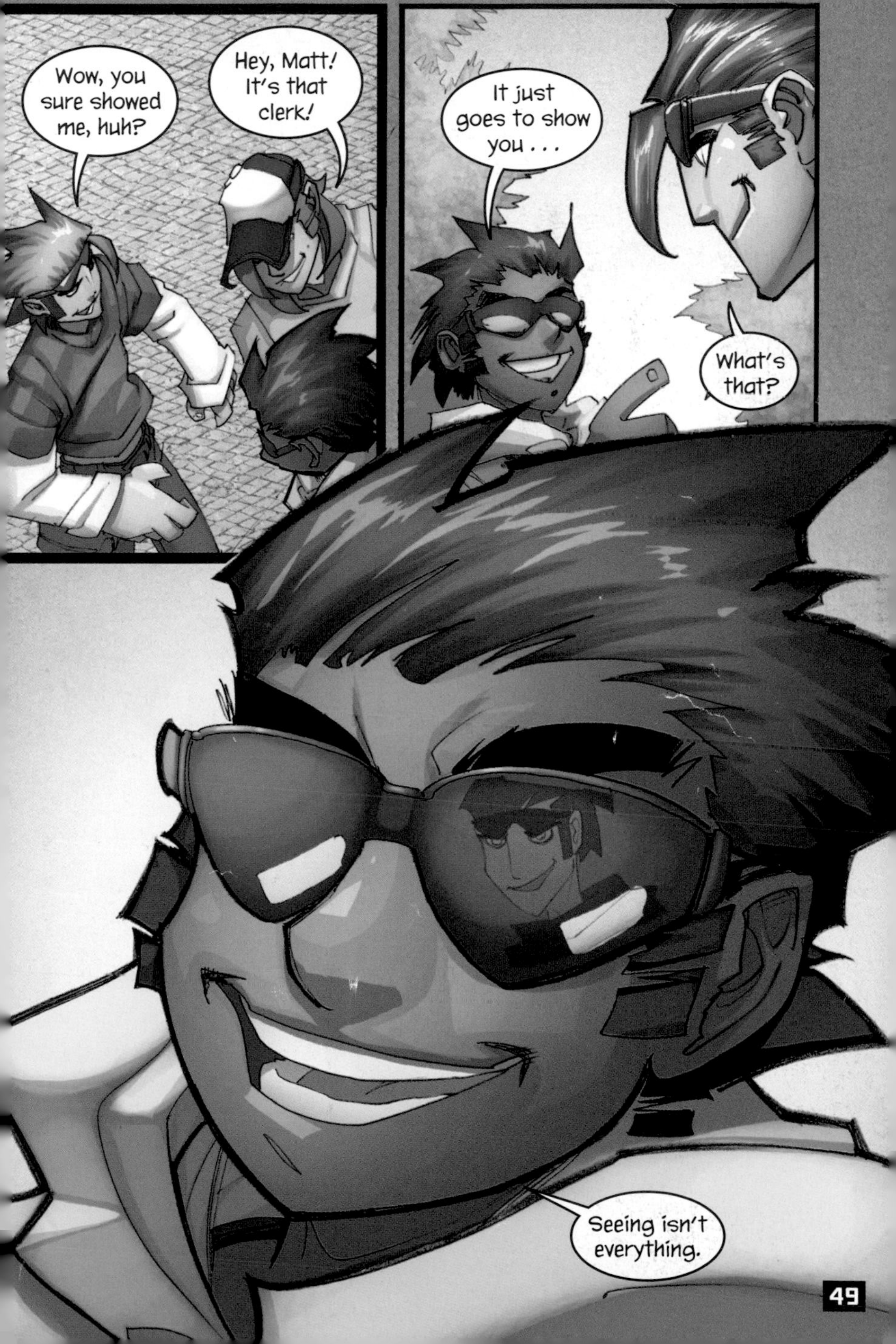
Wow, you sure showed me, huh?
Hey, Matt! It's that clerk!
It just goes to show you . . .
What's that?
Seeing isn't everything.

SPORTS ZONE

POSTGAME RECAP

SKT
SKATEBOARDING

PNT
PAINTBALL

FBL
FOOTBALL

BSL
BASEBALL

BBL
BASKETBALL

HKY

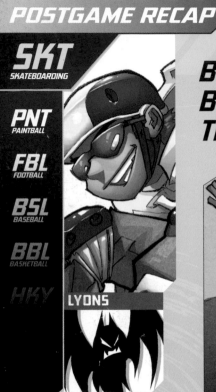

LYONS

BLIND SKATER BEATS BULLY BOARDER ON THE STREET COURSE!

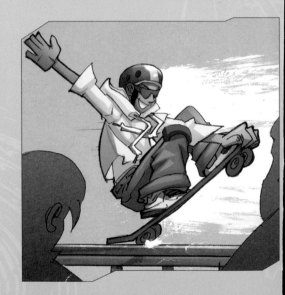

BY THE NUMBERS

STREET COURSE:
MATTY: 9.0, 9.7
BING: 9.1, 9.3

HALFPIPE:
TY: 8.8, 9.1
CLINT: 8.9, 8.9

STORY: Six-time street course champion, Bing Hawtin, finally met his match earlier today when blind skater, Matthew Lyons, took home the All-City trophy. Matty earned many new fans in his two routines for his creativity and technical skill. When asked how he felt about being a blind skater, Matt was quoted as saying that "seeing isn't everything".

Sports Illustrated KIDS

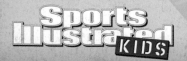

UP NEXT: SI KIDS INFO CENTRE

BLZ vs BHS
3-1
TGR vs ROR
33-32
EAG vs BAN
14-7
SPA vs WLD
4-3
BAN vs BHS
21-15
ROR vs LIG
4-3
BLZ vs BHS
3-1

Skateboarding fans got a real treat today when Matty one-upped skateboard bully Bing Hawtin, on the street course. Let's go into the stands and ask some fans for their opinions on the day's events ...

DISCUSSION QUESTION 1

Matty is blind, but he didn't let his disability prevent him from skateboarding. If you were blind, how would your life be different? How would it be the same?

DISCUSSION QUESTION 2

Ty Taggart had some trouble managing his anger. What do you do when you get angry? Can anger ever be a good thing? Why or why not?

WRITING PROMPT 1

Bing the bully is out to get Matt and Ty. Have you ever had to deal with a bully? What happened? Write about your bully experience.

WRITING PROMPT 2

Matty and Ty win the street course and halfpipe competitions, respectively. Have you ever competed for something? What happened? Write about it.

INFO CENTRE

GLOSSARY

AIR if you grab air, you are riding with all four skateboard wheels off the ground

CONDUCT behaviour

ECHOLOCATION method of locating something by determining the time for an echo to return to its source, such as with radar or sonar

GRAB holding on to your skateboard and striking a pose in mid-air

GRIND skating with one or both axles of your board on a kerb, railing or other surface

HALFPIPE U-shaped ramp of any size, usually with a flat section in the middle, that is used for skateboarding

JERK someone who is foolish or mean

KINDERGARTEN another word for pre-school or nursery

SIGHTED able to see

UNSPORTSMANLIKE not displaying the behaviour of a good sport, or to play dirty

CREATORS

ERIC STEVENS › Author

Eric Stevens lives in Minnesota, USA. He is studying to become an English teacher. His favourite things include pizza, video games, watching cooking programmes on TV, riding his bike and trying new restaurants. Some of his least favourite things include olives and shovelling snow.

GERARDO SANDOVAL › Illustrator

Gerardo Sandoval is a professional comic book illustrator from Mexico. He has worked on many well-known comics including the Tomb Raider books from Top Cow Productions. He has also worked on designs for posters and card sets.

BENNY FUENTES › Colourist

Benny Fuentes lives in Villahermosa, Tabasco in Mexico, where it's just as hot as the sauce is. He studied graphic design at college, but now he works as a full-time colourist in the comic book industry for companies such as Marvel, DC Comics and Top Cow Productions. He shares his home with two crazy cats, Chelo and Kitty.

>> LOVE THIS QUICK COMIC? READ THE WHOLE STORY IN
POINT-BLANK PAINTBALL

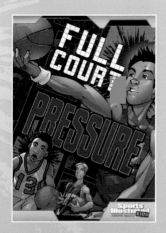

HOT SPORTS. HOT FORMAT!

PAINTBALL PUNK
Sports Illustrated KIDS
GRAPHIC NOVELS

Sports Illustrated KIDS
GRAPHIC NOVELS
BMX BLITZ

TRACK TEAM TITANS
Sports Illustrated KIDS
GRAPHIC NOVELS

FULL COURT FLASH
Sports Illustrated KIDS
GRAPHIC NOVELS

RIPTIDE PRIDE
Sports Illustrated KIDS
GRAPHIC NOVELS

Sports Illustrated KIDS
GRAPHIC NOVELS
BMX BREAKTHROUGH

Sports Illustrated KIDS
GRAPHIC NOVELS

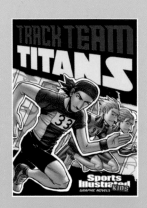

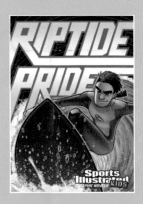

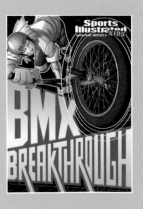